MAKE MY BED
IN HELL

Books by John Sanford

The Old Man's Place
The People from Heaven
A Man Without Shoes
The Land that Touches Mine
Every Island Fled Away
The $300 Man
A More Goodly Country
Adirondack Stories
View from this Wilderness
To Feed Their Hopes
The Winters of that Country
William Carlos Williams/John Sanford: A Correspondence
The Color of the Air
The Waters of Darkness
A Very Good Land to Fall Wit
A Walk in the Fire
The Season, It Was Winter
Maggie: A Love Story,
The View from Mt. Morris
We Have a Little Sister
Intruders in Paradise
A Palace of Silver
Speaking in an Empty Room: The Selected Letters of John Sanford

As Julian L. Shapiro

The Water Wheel

MAKE MY BED
IN HELL

JOHN SANFORD

BOOKS

ISBN-13: 978-1-7358517-2-3

Published by
Brash Books
PO Box 8212
Calabasas, CA 91372
www.brash-books.com

For MARGUERITE

"If I ascend up into heaven, thou art there: If I make my bed in hell, behold, thou art there."
Psalm 139.8

PUBLISHER'S NOTE

I t is a pleasure to bring back into print a crime-writing masterpiece—*Make My Bed in Hell* by John Sanford. This hardboiled classic, originally published in 1939, showcases Sanford as a supreme stylist. He heightens the effect of his language by combining words in unusual ways, such as "nickelplate" or "burntmatch." In addition, *Make My Bed in Hell* alternates between three narrative voices, each contributing a different perspective to the story. Late in the novel, Sanford includes a historical poem, focused on America's bloody past, that gives a foundation for the novel's events. While these artistic elements may initially surprise readers, they will enhance and deepen the overall reading experience. John Sanford has been described as America's "most outstanding neglected novelist." With this Brash Books edition, we aim to end this neglect!

✤ ✤ ✤

At five o'clock in the morning, Platt floated up to the surface of sleep—slowly, like a drowned man, sprawling—and then, awake, he tossed aside the horseblankets that covered him and climbed out of bed. Fumbling with himself through his mealy underwear, raking the coarse wool from his armpits, his crotch, and the hard apple of his backside, he hobbled to a window, melted away a section of the pinetree pattern of frost, and squinted down at the farmyard.

A last thin silt of flakes still tumbled in the quiet air. The snowfall had begun the day before, and now everything horizontal bore a twofoot smother, all of it gray in the gray morning. Platt shivered as his sleepcandied eyelids scratched the slate of the landscape. He turned away from the window, hugging the bags of his underwear against his body; before him was the scarecrow of clothes that he had built on one of the bedposts.

Dressed, he went downstairs to the kitchen. Laying the makings of a fire in the woodstove, he doused them with kerosene and flicked a lighted match across the open lid. The ignited vapor bloomed in a panic of flames that crawled all over each other in the frenzy of escape. Platt quelled them with a waterkettle, and taking up a couple of milkpails, he kicked his way into a drift that almost blocked the door.

The farmhouse lay near the bottom of a longsweeping grade. Above it, beyond a shallow sink, the barn rose flatly, like a photograph of itself, and on a line with the barn, forming the third corner of a triangle of buildings, stood a foursquare privy. Halfway

1

up the slope, the great nervous system of a solitary elm flowed into the churning sky.

On his way to the privy Platt came upon a wavering trail of footprints. The tracks roved uncertainly, going forward a few yards and then making a sudden aimless veer, and twice looping back on themselves over level clearings. Behind the barn, near the hillside runway, Platt found the deep intaglio of an entire body. Drops of blood had melted little pockmarks into the snow-cast of the face.

The sliding door was partly open. Platt entered the barn, and after kicking about in the haypiles, he went down a short corridor fronting four stalls. There were workhorses in the first two, and the third was empty. Flat on his back in the last one, a man lay sleeping in the stale straw bedding.

Platt looked down at him for a moment, and then suddenly he bashed the milkpails against the wall. The horses were frightened by the loud tinsound in the stillness of the barn; they bucked away from their cribs, pounding their hoofs on the planking of the partition. The sleeping man did not move.

Grabbing one of the outflung arms, Platt twisted it until it stiffened; then, watching the man's face, he slowly put on the pressure. The man stirred a little, as if the mounting pain, blunted by many hours of sleep, were only being dreamed of. Platt gave the arm another wrench, this time with more power.

The man opened his eyes very carefully, as if he were afraid they would roll off his face if he raised the lids too far. The inflamed little balls were wobbling marbles, streaked like reals with wisps of red. It was several seconds before the man succeeded in fixing them on Platt, and when he did, a vague expression rose to his face and began to take shape at the ends of his mouth. The eyes turned turtle almost at once, however, and the lids came down and covered them, and the expression, still meaningless, was gone.

Platt released the man's arm. It flopped like a length of rubber hose, arranging itself a little, expanding, and then it lay still. Platt went down a steep flight of steps to the cowshed ... .

⚜   ⚜   ⚜

Jessup: ... You say it was cold in the barn, Mister Platt. *How cold?*

Platt: Cold enough to freeze the snot in your nose. I seen it get pretty bad around Warrensburg in my time, but never like it was that morning. The cows was steaming like they'd come to a boil, and the trough in back of them was choked with dumps of frozen manure that you couldn't of busted up without a pickaxe.

Jessup: You're talking about the cowshed. How was it up above, where Paulhan was lying?

Platt: Even colder. Down in the cowshed you get the body-heat of the stock.

Jessup: Did Paulhan have any covering on him when you found him in the empty stall?

Platt: Nothing but his clothes.

Jessup: What was he wearing?

Platt: A knit cap that come down over his ears, a short coat reaching about halfway to his knees, pants made out of some light kind of stuff, no boots, only that thin pair of low shoes. There was a couple of horseblankets on the wall right above him, but it must of been dark when he come in the barn, and I guess he didn't see them, or else he was so done in that he couldn't pull them off the pegs.

Jessup: What did you do when you saw him?

Platt: Nothing.

Jessup: You didn't even put the blankets over him?

Platt: What for? Nobody sent for him, and nobody was holding him there in my barn. It was a little after five in the morning the first time I seen him there, and I was on my way to milk the cows. I tried to wake him up, but he couldn't hardly open his eyes,

3

let alone stand on his feet, so I let him lay where he was while I went about my chores. There wasn't any call for me to go back to the barn during the day, so I didn't see him again till that night.

Jessup: You didn't go back to see how he was? You didn't go back to the barn all day long—from five in the morning to nightfall?

Platt: That's right. I didn't see Paulhan again till just before supper . . . .

⚜　⚜　⚜

When Platt had finished milking the cows, he forked some cornstalks over to the yokes, picked up the pails, and left the shed. Dumping all but a couple of quarts of the milk into the snow, he returned to the house and began to prepare his breakfast.

He took a blackened iron spider from the oven, covered the bottom with slabs of salt pork, and set it on the stove. Then he sliced some cold potatoes into the crackling fat, and while they were frying, he poured some hot water into a pot, added a few spoonfuls of coffee to it, and stirred it over the open fire until it foamed up to the brim. Now he broke four eggs over the potatoes and the rippling strips of pork, and when the omelet had coagulated, he scraped it onto a large plate. Carrying this and the coffeepot to the kitchen table, he sat down to his meal. He worked steadily and quickly, taking only three or four minutes to eat the omelet and the several chunks of bread that he used for mopping up the hardening grease.

After a second cup of coffee, he loaded a pipe with crumbled plug, and then for a long time he stared at the eyes of the stove, listening to the firecracker fire of dry timber, the distant tumult of flames snapping off short in the base of the chimney. For a long time he sat there, his pipesmoke surging above him in chiffon streamers—and suddenly he thought of the man in the barn.

He rose from his chair and moved idly about the room, touching objects as he passed them without knowing what they were or why they had attracted his hands—and the face of the man in the barn was in the frostferns covering the windowpanes, in the waterstains on the ceiling, in the fuzz of carbon that coated the faded designs of the wallpaper.

Platt's wandering came to an end before a closed door. Finding the lock frozen with rust, he twisted the key until the bolt worked loose from its scab of corrosion and screeched back into the slot. He entered the darkened room and tried to roll up one of the shades, but the dead linen tore loose from its spool and fell sandsounding to the floor.

On the wall near the mantelpiece hung a large advertising calendar. Under its lithograph—a pharmacist impaling the world on a moxie stare—was pasted a little pamphlet of months beginning with May, and at the bottom, in great numerals, was the date of issue: 1923. Platt was in the parlor of the farmhouse for the first time in sixteen years.

Mice had gnawed into the upholstery of a green plush sofa. From the hole boiled a giant fungus of yellow stuffing, and shreds of this made a trail that traversed the carpet and disappeared under the door of a cupboard. Here, on the bedrock of a family Bible, Platt found the spongy nest of the mice, speckled everywhere with their little bullet droppings. As deep as *Deuteronomy*, solid pages of the Bible were discolored by seepage from the nest, but successive filtrations had made the stain noticeably fainter at *Ezra*, and beyond the first few chapters of *Lamentations* it was no longer visible.

Platt turned to the Record. On the lefthand page was a single entry:

Amram Platt & Eliz. Bolton
maried 14 Mch 1890.

On the opposite page were listed the given names of their six children, together with the dates of birth and death:

5

Matthew—20 Jany 1891 : 3 Aug 1896
Miriam—29 Decbr 1891 : 11 Jany 1892
Henrietta—16 Feby 1893 : 10 Aug 1896
Andrew—5 Apr 1894 : 1 Decbr 1902
Theodore—15 June 1895 : 18 Mch 1900
Aaron—5 July 1900 :

All these entries, and another concerning the death of his wife in 1915, had been made by Amram Platt. A final note was in Aaron's handwriting:

4 May 1923—My father died
today. I am glad he died. He
was a nogood sonofabitch.

Sixteen years of dust lay on the potbelly of the Dresden tablelamp. The copper jugs at the ends of the mantelpiece were coated with an icing of pistache mold, and between them, almost hidden by its cassock of dusty glass, stood a gilt clock that had stopped with its hands outstretched at a quarter to three. Over the cupboard hung an oakframed photograph of Elizabeth and Amram Platt, their faces concealed now by a panel of wallpaper that had furled down from the molding. In her dim hands the woman held a dim book against the tight bodice of a dress that compressed her like a broom; the man wore a highbuttoned frock coat with facings of satin, and on the crook of his right arm a silk hat squatted like a demijohn....

❧   ❧   ❧

His oil lamp shuttling a smear of light on the gunmetal snow, Platt returned to the barn late in the afternoon. He found Paulhan awake now and covered with one of the horseblankets.

"What the hell are you doing in my barn?" Platt said.

Paulhan stared up at the oscillating shadows among the rafters.

"If you don't want to talk, you can pick up your ass and start traveling again. What the hell are you doing in my barn?"

"Resting," Paulhan said, his voice sounding like a wind moving among dry leaves. "Resting."

"You picked out the wrong place. This barn's no comfort station for every panhandler that takes a notion to drop in."

"You can only eat one meal at a time."

"What?"

"You can only eat one meal at a time."

"You always get hungry again, though."

"That's the time to worry your head."

"That's the time *you* worry it! When *I* want to eat, first I got to take the food and wash my sweat off of it, or else I got to pay hard money for the right to dig it out of a can."

"Why don't you let go of the dirty end of the stick?"

"Yours is dirtier, you bastard! When'd you do your last day's work?"

"Oh, Christ, I forget—years and years ago."

"You got your brass to talk like that, being on the bum all your life."

"The one on the dirty end always makes the same old beef."

Platt shifted his weight to the left leg, measuring the distance between his right foot and Paulhan's mouth.

Paulhan looked up at him. "Anyway, what're *you* so sure about? What do *you* care how I live?"

Platt spoke to the man's mouth, not his eyes. "A whole lot," he said. "I bitched my life away on this pile of stones, and it don't make me feel any better to hear you blow about taking your case while I was doing it. It looks like you got winning ways."

"I get by," Paulhan said. "The decent folk chip in, and the tightwads don't. Whenever the door slams in my face, I just keep on moving...." His voice began to fade now. "There are other people around, everywhere you turn. The world's full of people...."

After taking care of the stock, Platt went back to the house and made supper. It was bedtime when he had finished washing the dishes....

❧ ❧ ❧

Platt: ... I don't know how he got the blanket down off of the wall. I told you I didn't go near the barn all day.

Jessup: Did he talk to you when you saw him that afternoon?

Platt: Yes.

Jessup: What about?

Platt: The way he'd been getting along. I asked him when he done his last day's work, and he said he couldn't remember. All the time he was knocking around the world I was busting my God damn heart on that quarry of mine, so fagged out some nights that I'd fall asleep with my face in the dirty plates on the kitchen table. If I was like Paulhan, I'd of been sporting under the bedclothes instead of squatting out in the cold just to yank at a cow's tit; I'd of lazed around till the cows milked theirselves before I went out and froze my nuts off for them.

Jessup: I didn't ask you what you'd have done if you were Paulhan. I just want to know what he said to you.

Platt: If you don't like the way I'm telling this, you can go stick your fingers in your ears.

Jessup: No sense getting on your high horse, Mister Platt. I'm only trying to tell you....

Platt: You only ask the questions. I'm the one does the telling.

Jessup: Then why are you beating around the bush?

Platt: Because I got something on my mind that I been waiting years to pass along to all these rockfaced bastards setting out here in front of us. I been saving up a story for them ever since

I was a kid, and this is the best chance to tell it that's come my way so far.

Jessup: I don't see what your childhood's got to do with this Paulhan business.

Platt: Maybe not, but you will by the time I get done. You want to listen?

Jessup: Go ahead.

Platt: I'm the only one of Amram Platt's children that grew up, but if you think he was any softer with me on that account, you got another guess coming to you. Nobody in Christ's world ever got any kindness out of him, and me being the only one left out of his six tries for a set of farmhands didn't get me any special favors. It only got me the work that belonged to the dead ones.

You couldn't fool around with Amram Platt any more than the ass end of a mule. If you wanted to eat, first off you had to sweat—and you done that till it run down in your eyes, till you could of wrang a quart of it out of your clothes, till your boots and socks got so soggy with it that you felt like you was walking barefoot in mud.

That's the kind of treatment I had from the time I was eight years old, and it didn't make any neverminds to the old man if I was so sick that I couldn't hardly stand on my feet. I can remember days when I got up in the morning with such an ache in my head that my brains felt like they was going to blow off the top of my skull, but little things like that didn't keep me laying around in bed. What the hell did my old man care about headaches, pains in the back, fevers, chills, sore throats? What the hell did he care if you scalded yourself with boiling fat, or if you was hacking up chunks of phlegm like tadpoles? You *worked,* and it wouldn't of made any difference to him if you busted your leg, or the horse went and booted your balls all the way up to your Adam's apple.

You hear plenty of stories about a farmer has a good life, but the people that tell them don't know their hole from a horsecollar. By the time they get done passing that elegant talk, you'd think that all there was to farming was sprinkling a handful of seeds on the ground and letting God do the rest. The only trouble is God don't do you a God damn bit of good; He only makes it harder. He gives you a drought when you're begging for rain, and when He finally turns on the rain, He makes it a flood. You get down on your knees, and you pray like hell for just a little shower, and what does He do but get gay and try to drown you out?

It's all right for the rich man, the slob that comes up in his big automobile and watches you plug along in back of a plow. From where he's resting his fat, the fields look nice and pretty, and the furrows all even and straight, and you're having the time of your life out there in the boiling sun. But just let the bastard step out of that automobile and dirty his shoeleather a little—the ground won't look so pretty when he gets his snotter right down close to it. With all them rocks and weeds and roots, it won't look any more like you went and drew the furrows with your fingertips....

⚜ ⚜ ⚜

It was colder in the morning. A steady wind shot down the hillside, planing the corrugations off the snow and piling drifts against every object that broke its long curving sweep. Finding the waterbucket a great candle of ice, Platt filled the kettle with snow, and after making a fire, he slogged his way to the barn.

Paulhan was asleep. Platt put the sole of his boot on the man's curled fingers and pressed down until the joints cracked. Paulhan opened his eyes and slowly turned to his deadened hand, looking at it as if it belonged to someone else, as if it were not a hand at all, but a partly crushed insect. He spoke to the groping ruin.

—It was one of those cheap little dumps....

He smiled, and then he stopped smiling. The expression came and went so quickly that it seemed to have been nothing more than a muscular twitch. Platt watched him for a while, saying nothing, and finally Paulhan spoke, broke into the middle of an idea and spoke, as if he were reading the words from the top of a page come upon at random.

—... and on the stairs, the canter of heels, and she went out toward the middle of the floor, not walking, not just walking, but flowing like a comber, and the spotlight flowed with her over the boards, washing across her feet and marooning her on a drifting island, and the crowd came up like a wave breaking on rocks— and then the writhing spiral music, wrapping itself around ....

—... a pout of flesh that he pinched up from my forearm, and I heard the rubbery puncture not with my ears, but my blood, and he shot the plunger down a little too fast, the jet of liquid cysting under the skin ....

—... and slowly she began to flirt the carnation of her dress, a dozen kneehigh skirts amberswirling, and she wore umber shoes, and her smokesilk stockings boomed up and disappeared into the eddying flower ....

—... but not your hands, not your hands—your *mouth!* You wanted to attack her with your teeth, sink them into her body, stuff yourself with her flesh. You couldn't stand having some part of her left outside of you—but you wanted to use your mouth, your mouth ....

—... played with the floating plate of light, flashing over it so fast that her skirts came to a boil, chattering the wooden shells until they stuttered like drumfire, now and then stamping her heels so hard that long gray combs of dust sprang from between the floorboards ....

—... and very slow now, the music was, gnashing, and I sat there watching the woman and wiping my palms on the table-cloth, over and over again slowly wiping them on the tablecloth, and then the music slashed up to one last tearing jerking tincan smash, the woman's body cakewalking in the final orgasms of a mechanical jigger running down—and it was over.

—... slamming their chairs on the floor, trembling it like a cavalcade galloping over a wooden bridge, and firefly coins spun out of the darkness, and folded bills flew into the lightcone and dropped dead around her feet like a shower of scorched moths, and for a moment she stood where she was ....

—... and the boy stooped to gather the money for her, and then she dropped her arms, waiting for him to hand her the red velvet bag ....

—... watching her go off, and then all of a sudden she turned and came back, came back to my table and sat down, looking at me. Scooping out my handful of centavos, I smeared them across my palm. Still looking at me, she took a bill from the bag and tossed it over my beerglass. It landed in my lap. Fifty pesetas, it called for, and I ordered wine ....

—... flicked the bag with her finger, saying, 'Some day I will be finished with dancing for copper. Some day I will be in Paris, in Roma, in Nev York.'

—I said, 'What're you waiting for? If you ever dance like that in Paris, they'll stuff goldpieces down your throat.'

—She shook her head, saying, 'I will go when I am ready to go, when I have enough money so that no man can say to me that I must dance for him on my back before he will let me dance for him on my feet.'

—The music started again. This time it was a paso doble, and ....

—... staring at the scrap of paper propped against the water-pitcher, fingering the little spongy bulge under the skin of my forearm, thinking that I ought to crumple the paper into a ball and spick it away from me and forget about it, but knowing all the time that I'd never be able to do that, *knowing* it ....

—... was still fine outside, and still early, only about two o'clock, and the Ramblas was still packed. I crossed to the middle walk and headed for the Plaza de Cataluna, and as far up the street as I could see there were little stands where they sold butts, birds, flowers, bombones, bullfight tickets, and I walked through bank after bank of flowersmells, looking at the men and women all around me, on the sidewalks, in the gutters, leaning over balconies, sitting on the tops of streetcars, and I saw soldiers with burlap uniforms and canvas sandals, and Civil Guards monkeyfaced under their patentleather hats, and girls with crockery skin and hair like lacquer, and bucks watching the girls pass by and gently calling, 'Guapa! Guapa!' and skinny little kids hollering, 'Bombones! Informaciones! Bombones! Informaciones!' and mingling with everything was the cawcawchorus from five thousand birdcages, and finally, adding my own laughter to the great gay uproar, I gave up trying to figure out whether I was in a zoo or a jungle or a street carnival—I just looked at the people, sniffed in the smells, listened to the sounds....

—... and bought the woman a bottle of Grand Marnier with her own money, and up where the Ramblas opens into the Plaza I stopped a cab and gave the piece of paper to the driver, and we were on our way, making a left turn into the Paseo de Gracia and staying on it for miles. It was one of those bluedust nights, full of faraway stars that gave the sky a satin frosting....

—... and rapped on a panel. The sound broke ironbarrel loud in the empty silent street, and when the door was opened, I offered the Grand Marnier to the darkness as if it were a torch. I saw only a dim face, disembodied and tired, smeared a little, and then it sidled off and disappeared, and I heard slipperheels whacking away up the hall. I followed the sound, feeling my way with the bottle. The woman was waiting for me in the parlor....

—... trying to tell me that her cousin was in the house. She said, 'He come from Saragossa this afternoon to settle a business affair, and you will please do not notice the untidy way my house is.'

—I said....

—... we were passing the door when a backdraft sucked it open, and a wedge of light from the parlor was laid down across the bottom of a bed. A pair of pants on the brass railing, a pair of shoes on the floor, a pair of feet on the rumpled blankets....

—... and the aircurrent nudged the door back again, and the catch held. I put the bottle down on a table, carefully, intently, as if there were only one spot in the world that would hold it.

—She said, 'That is my cousin. He is resting after his long journey.'

—'And did he settle his business affair?'

—'Yes,' she said. 'The affair is settle....'

—... in another room, another bedroom, and I went to the window and stood there looking out, and the woman followed me and closed the door, letting the room stay dark. In the harbor there were single lights, double lights, little chains of lights on the water, so far away and down that I had to stare at them for a long time before I could tell whether they were moving. The woman was right behind me now, almost touching me, but I kept on looking out into the dark.

—She said, 'He pay me. He pay me much money. I do not refuse to see him.'

—'I *don't* pay.'

—'I will not always be at the *Olympia*. Some day I will be finish with dancing for centavos. Some day I will be in Paris, in Roma, in Nev York.'

—'You'll never get there with me.'

—'Soon I will not be at the *Olympia* any more. I have make a lot of money with dancing and with other things, and soon I will go away. It was different before. Then I would not even look at a man if he do not pay me first, but now I not always try to get money.'

—'How about your cousin from Saragossa?'

—She was standing so close to me that I could feel the vibration of her voice with the back of my neck. 'He is not my cousin,' she said. 'It was a lie when I say that he is my cousin—but it is not the same with him. He pay for this house, and also he pay money when he come here, and I do not refuse to see him. He is the one that was first with me, and so it is not the same. I too come from

Saragossa, and he was the first one, and always he will be able to see me, and always he will pay money because he was the first one, and I will never keep him out in my lifetime. That is the great punishment to him—that he must pay money to me—and I think he will not again do with other girls what he do with me when I am only eleven years old ....'

—... remembering the napoleon of leaves ashing underfoot, remembering the fernfountains in the shaded hollows, remembering the waves of wind sandancing in the trees, and I remembered too that the sun was going down into the hair of a ridge, and the light was screened thin by the pines, as if I were looking at it through my eyelashes—and it was the beginning of night for everything that lived in the woods.

—I listened, and after a long time the first nightsound filtered through the muslin air: on an alderbranch a thrush was making its serene and impersonal song, a fragile fifing, a clear woodround succession of tones. Very quietly and very slowly I raised the rifle, and so steady were my hands as I looked down the gunbarrel that the bird seemed to be perched on the forward sight. Tilting the muzzle a little, I cocked the hammer.

—From far off in the woods I heard a diminished reply to the song, and thinking of nothing but the fading distant music, I pulled the trigger. The bird sprayed its wings and tried to fly away—but once only. Its head fell like a locket against its chest, and the body sagged, the wings seeming to refold of themselves. For an instant the bird lay balanced on the branch, and then it toppled into the deep grass.

—I stood still, watching a slow streamer of gray smoke drift from the barrel of the rifle, wondering why I hadn't heard the explosion of the shot, why my tongue was pressed against the ceiling of my mouth, why my hands and arms and body were so rigid, why now time was tumbling in the air like snow.

—I picked up the bird. The pattern of feathers was unmarred, the fine stencil of brown figures on the white shield of the chest.

I heard the intermittent call of the other thrush, not more often repeated than before, not yet querying the silence of the dead bird, but still impersonal and serene.

—Eleven years old! *Eleven years old!* ...

—...and she said, 'He ask me now all the time to let him be my husband, but I will not do that because then he will be absolve, and he will forget the thing he do with me when I am only eleven years old. All his lifetime he will follow me—to Paris, to Roma, to Nev York, everywhere—and all his lifetime he will ask me to let him be my husband, even if my belly is fat like a clown with the child that is not his child, even if I am sick with the syphilis sickness, even if I am a dirty wrinkled old woman that has not a good smell in her mouth and between her legs, but I will never in my lifetime do what he ask. He is now only a good customer....'

—...and I heard the sound of silk rubbing on silk, of silk being bunched and thrown away, of silk hushing itself into silence as it slid along the floor, and feeling the shape of her body through the back of my coat, I tried my best to think of that little bump on my arm, but she pressed closer and closer to me, and finally I couldn't stand it any more, I couldn't stand it any more, *I couldn't stand it,* and I had to turn around ....

Paulhan's voice dwindled like steam. His eyes had closed while he was talking, and now every muscle relaxed, and his body seemed all at once to go to pieces. Platt stared down at him for a moment and then kicked him in the mouth. His head spun loosely around, snapped back, and lay still, and from his lower lip a worm of blood began to crawl across his face ....

⚜ ⚜ ⚜

Platt went up to the bedroom, moved about idly for a while, and came to a stop before a chiffonier that had belonged to his wife.

Holding the tarnished knobs of the top drawer, he tried vainly to recall what it contained. He opened the drawer.

In one of the compartments of a cedarwood box, he rediscovered a coiled braid of dark brown hair. In smaller compartments there were mufflike buns to match, but now as always it was the braid that fascinated him. He fingered it lightly and with distaste, but having touched it, he was forced to take it from the box. Holding the transformation by its thread buttonhole, he let it jiggle before him; it yawned up and down like a spent spring. He revolved it a few times, and then wondering what he would look like with a beard, he took a few steps toward a mirror. He stopped suddenly, remembering his wife, and he was so invaded by disgust that his stomach shrank like foam. Striking a match, he held it under the twisting hair. It went soaring up to nothing in a single gash of fire. He dropped the blaze to the floor and stamped on it, and when he removed his boot all that remained of the switch was its charred loop. Smelling like smoke from a dumpfire, a fine light haze rebounded gently from the ceiling.

Platt went back to the chiffonier and fumbled with the trinkets in the open drawer. There were a few combs and hairpins, some lengths of stiffened ribbon, a spool of elastic that broke like a woodshaving when he tried to unreel it, a sheaf of desiccated leather haircurlers, a lace choker ribbed with celluloid, a hank of corsetstring, a box of unscented rice powder now brown with mold, and a plate of false teeth for the upper jaw. Under the choker were three pennypostals, one of the Grand Union Hotel at Saratoga, one of the steamer *Sagamore* at the Lake George landing, and one of the cable railway on Mount Marcy.

Looking helplessly at this accumulation of junk as he sifted it with his fingers, he knew neither what to do with it nor how to escape it. It seemed to be clinging to him, hooking into his flesh with hundreds of minute sawtoothed legs. He felt as if he were being overrun by a horde of insects.

He remembered now the contents of the second drawer, and he knew without opening it precisely how each article was disposed, but he found it impossible to quit the room before completing the ritual of inspection. He opened the drawer and took a garment from one of the neat piles of clothing. It was a suit of his wife's underwear, heavy woolen underwear, its creased arms and legs dangling like those of a person who had been hanged. Slowly Platt turned it around. The long placket in the seat was still buttoned.

In a sudden desperate revolt, he ripped the underwear apart. At the first tug, the front buttons flew off from collar to crotch, and the back of the rotting fabric parted all the way down to the vent. Holding the sleeves, he stood on the rest of the suit and wrenched at it until it lay about him in rags. Then he turned and ran toward the door . . . .

⚜ ⚜ ⚜

Platt: . . . And all the time he was raving about this whoor from the dancehall, I was thinking about my prissy wife, a tall tight skinny frump with feet as cold as rocks and a build onto her like a disk harrow. All day long she walked around dressed in more damn clothes than ever you could stuff in a suitcase, and even when she went to bed she was still wearing most of the rig she fenced herself in with in the daytime. You couldn't of got to her without blasting, but she wasn't worth that kind of a fuss; she'd only of hollered blue murder and laid under you as stiff as a coldstorage beef, with her hands squeezing down on a pair of flabby little tits that hung off of her like pockets turned inside out. Hell, she wasn't worth rolling over for; you'd only of felt you was crawling on a bed filled with starched collars. I had five solid years of sleeping next to that iron windowdummy, five solid years of trying to warm up to the most righteous woman that ever walled herself up in a corset, and you're way far off if you think I felt any gladder about it after listening to Paulhan make his brags about this dancing whoor, and about how he went up to her house in the dead of night, and about how she stood up close to him in the bedroom with nothing in between him and her naked body but the back of his coat. God damn it! How much do you think a man can stand? ...

❧   ❧   ❧

Platt wandered about the now stultifying house until it seemed to shrink, until it focused upon him and converged, and at last, when he felt it impeding his movements, he went outside to avoid a blockade of objects—pots, dishes, boxes, furniture—that no effort of will could make him unaware of.

No snow fell now from the crumpled tinfoil clouds, but a hard flat wind broke the overhangs off the drifts and hammered them into Platt's face. A swarm of sparrows roosted on a bush near the woodshed. Expanded to keep out the cold, the birds transformed themselves into catkins and the bush into a clump of pussywillow. Suddenly one of them left its perch and flew from branch to branch, loudly abusing the others. Disturbed, all the birds began to quarrel, and then the entire mob blew up from the bush. Platt watched them swirl across the snow to a wire fence, where, deployed in single file, they looked like clothespins on a line.

Beyond the fence was the barn ....

❧   ❧   ❧

—... The first real toy I ever had was a set of tin trains. You wound up the engine with a key that stuck out of the firebox under the roof of the cab, and you coupled it with a tender that was covered with a lumpy sheet of blackpainted tin supposed to be a load of coal, and then you pulled up the catch in the smokestack, and off the cars went around a little beltline of tin track.

—For the first few circuits, they traveled so fast that they almost derailed themselves, but after that the spring in the engine began to run down, and the cars went more and more slowly until they were just creeping along the track; and when they came to a standstill, and you picked up the engine to give it another winding, you were always a little startled to find that the drivers still had a few kicks left in them, and they buzzed your fingers like a vibrator until the motor was all played out.

—I never tired of that toy. I worked it day in and day out for a couple of years, and long after the cars had gotten lost, after someone had stepped on the tender and sprung it so that it didn't fit the tracks, even after the engine had dwindled to a bare motor carried by two pairs of trucks, I kept on making believe that the toy was as good as new, that the paint was still unscratched, that the cars were still racing around the bends filled with the lead soldiers and sugarcubes that I used for passengers and baggage.

—Then one day we moved, and when my mother unpacked our things in the new house she couldn't find any of the tracks for my little set of trains. Only the brokendown engine was left, stripped of its boiler and cab and tender, without its cowcatcher, even without the key to its motor. I felt bad when I fumbled with the remnant of my railroad, not because I knew at last that it was only a toy, but because I saw for the first time that it was broken. As long as it ran, as long as there was some life in it, I hadn't cared about its appearance, but it was dead now, and it couldn't move, and there was no way to avoid seeing that it was a pretty sadlooking piece of junk.

—I tried my best to bring it back to life. I pushed it along the floorboards and the patterns in the carpet, I tied a string to it and dragged it after me over all the obstacles I could find, I slid it down every sloping surface in the house, but I was never able to fool myself: the engine was broken.

—I got angry with it because I couldn't make it run by itself, and I smashed it to bits with a hammer, but when I was all finished wrecking it, when the few remaining parts were lying scattered around me—the uncoiled spring, the dented casing plates, the twisted wheels—I suddenly began to cry....

⚜   ⚜   ⚜

Platt: ... I had a toy once, but it didn't come readymade from any store; I built it myself out of an old box I found in the woodshed. It was just an ordinary little box, without paint and lacking one of the ends, but it caught my eye, and I picked it up off a pile of kindling and turned it over and over in my hands, wondering what I could do with it. Finally I hit on the idea of making a wagon, and not having any knife of my own, I had to sneak my father's out of the kitchen and use it while he was working in the fields.

The hardest part of the carving job was making the wheels, and without that sharp knife I'd never of been able to round them out or give them a flat rolling edge. As it was, they turned out something dandy, and the next thing I had to do was cut a pair of axles, but alongside of shaping the wheels that wasn't hardly any trick at all. I tacked the axles onto the bottom of the box, and then I started boring holes in the wheels so's I could slip them over the hubs.

We didn't have any brace and bit around the farm, and I had to gouge out them holes with the point of the knife. Everything went along fine till I got to doing the last wheel, and then I found there was a knot in the wood right where the axle had to go through it. Twisting the knife around in that knot was mighty ticklish business, and I tried my damnedest to be careful about it, but luck was against me, and just as the point was coming through the far side of the knot, the blade caught in the toughest part of the grain, and the tip snapped off.

I was scared stiff about what my father'd do when he found out, but I was so close to the finish of the job that I kept right on with it, and in no time the wheel was ready. I didn't need the knife any more, so I put it back where it came from, hoping all the while that my father wouldn't notice the busted blade, and then I went outside again and put the last touches on the wagon. I fitted the wheels onto the axles, and by the time I'd fastened them in place with little cotter pins that I made out of wire, I was so proud of the job that I clean forgot about what I done to the knife.

Every kid acts just about the same when he's got a toy that strikes his fancy. He'll take the sorriest throwtogether of wood and string and wire, and make believe it's the genuine article. Paulhan wasn't any exception with them trains of his, and neither was I with my homemade wagon.

I hitched myself to it with a hunk of clothesline, and all day long I marched around the farm, tugging the toy along in back of me. I played all kinds of games with it. I loaded it with gravel and dumped the stuff in holes, making out I was repairing the roads; I filled it with twigs, and all at once I turned out to be a woodsman going down to Warrensburg with an order of lumber; I picked a wagonful of chokeberries, and the chokeberries was beets that I raised in my own truckgarden. I went out in the fields, fording the brook and hauling the wagon after me over the steepest slopes, and then I was horse and driver at one and the same time, and we was crossing the mountains bound for the goldmines in California, and we was set on by wild Indians a couple of times, and naturally I had to shoot my way out of being scalped by all them painted savages that was riding around and around me, firing their rifles, yelling like crazy, taking my hat off time and again with their poisontipped arrows.

I had one grand time that day. I got so wrapped up in that little wagon that I wouldn't of parted with it for anything in feathers, fur, or flannel, not because it was worth a good God damn, but because I'd made it myself. It wasn't only a toy to me; it was a contraption I'd put together out of pretty near nothing; I'd worked on it; I'd put something on the face of the earth that wasn't there before; and I had some of the feeling a man gets when he builds a house with his own hands. I wasn't but five or six at the time, but you don't have to be wearing any twofoot beard to get the notion I'm talking about.

Along about sundown I come out of the fields, and I was heading for the barn to put the wagon up just like a real one, but no sooner was I in sight of the house than I heard my father calling me. I went on down to see what he wanted, all the time harnessed to the wagon and practically walking backwards so's I could admire the way it rolled. My father was standing in the kitchen doorway. When I got to the foot of the stoop, he pulled his hand out of his pocket, and there was the busted knife.

It'd passed so clean out of my mind that when I seen it again it took me like a good swift kick in the bellybutton; my guts yawned wide open like a mouth.

My father said, "You been stinking around with this knife again?"

"Yes," I said.

"Why?"

"I was carving out something."

"And what was you carving out?"

"Oh, just something."

"What was you carving out?" he said. "You better talk up if you don't want a good belt in the mouth."

I seen there wasn't any help for it, so I said, "I was carving out them wheels," and I pointed at the wagon, but the words wasn't any sooner out of my mouth than I knew I'd made a big mistake.

He said, "Carving out them wheels, eh! So that's what you went and done after me telling you time and time again I didn't want you using my knife!" And down he come out of the doorway till he was standing right up against me and bulging out overhead like a tree.

I said, "I didn't mean to bust the knife, pa. Honest I didn't. It was just a accident."

"I'll learn you all about accidents, you little farthandle!" he
said, and he took his hand and clouted me such a beaut alongside
of the jaw that I piled up with my face in the dirt. "Accidents!"
he said, pulling back his foot and kicking the little wagon twenty
feet up in the air.

I heard the sound of smashing wood when he booted it, and
I heard another clatter when it hit the ground, but I didn't look
right away because all of a sudden my father started in to laugh.
He laughed like he'd heard the funniest joke in the world, a
joke that hit him in just the right spot, and out of that wideopen
mouth of his come the loudest braying and bellowing that I ever
heard from man or beast. It cracked him in half at the belly, and
there he squatted roaring that nasty laugh till he lost his breath
and started to choke.

That stopped him in a hurry, and when he got his wind back
he said, "After this you'll be keeping your hands off of my knife,"
and then he walked away.

I got up and went over to where the wagon was laying. Both
sides and the bottom was all stove in, and there was only one
wheel left onto the axles, and even that was cracked. I looked
down at the busted little toy that I'd had so much fun making
and playing with, but all the fun was very far away now, so far
that I couldn't hardly believe I'd ever had it. The bashedin slabs
of wood, the split axles, the flattened wheels—all that junk used
to belong to somebody else, not me. I let it lay there, and I went
away without once looking around, and I never found out what
become of it because I never went back to see. To this very day,
whenever I have to go near the spot, I always turn my head and
look another way....

❧ ❧ ❧

It was late afternoon when Platt left the barn, and for the first
time in three days he saw a rip in the booming cauliflower clouds.

The sun was behind a hill now, its ocher burst of light staining the edges of the hole in the sky. Platt went into the house and sat down near a window to watch the last faint colors dissolve in the creeping overwhelm of evening, and when in the glass before him he could see only the glowing face of the stove, he turned to it, removed one of the lids, and stared for a long time at graying coals over which sudden forays of flame rippled like pennants.

He had eaten nothing since early morning. Rebuilding the fire, he prepared a meal, and he was about to start eating when he felt his hunger clench. The food was gray: the stale fried pork looked like a slab of shale, the moldy rye bread was a longcold clinker, the boiled potatoes were stones, and the gravy paraffin. And the cutlery, from which the nickelplate had worn away, was lead, and the china, its glaze chipped off, was clay, and under both the oilcloth showed blotches of its canvas base. And the woodwork was dead, dry, withered, and Platt's fingernails were scored like clamshells, and his boots, socks, pants, shirt, hair .... Gray, all of it! The *world* was gray! He stood up and looked slowly about the kitchen. His eyes settled on the door to the yard .....

He entered the stall and lay down on a pile of straw near Paulhan, covering himself with the other blanket. He wondered how long Paulhan had been talking ....

⚜   ⚜   ⚜

—... We drove there the first day. It wasn't far from where we lived, only a couple of miles down the river road, but my father wanted to make sure that I'd know the way home. When we reached the school, he lifted me from the carriage and walked with me as far as the door, and then we shook hands, and he went away. I stood on the steps, watching him drive off, and once, up near the bend in the road, he looked back. We waved to each other, and then he was gone.

—The schoolyard was quiet. I heard the teacher's voice through the open windows, but it seemed even more distant than the chinasound of the Schroon giggling over the gravel shallows. I saw the river through the trees, and the sunlight shuttling on it made the wet stones and moving water look like broken glass. At the edge of the clearing I spotted a squirrel faking prayers as it spurted toward the end of a log. It never got there. From the beech overhead, a stooping sharpshin fell upon it like a piece of scrapiron, the wingbeats sounding like the opening of many umbrellas. Caught in the grapnels of the hawk, the squirrel made a long thindrawn cry, and as the bird flew out of sight among the trees the cry died away, and then once more it was quiet in the schoolyard.

—I didn't know what to do with myself after the door had closed behind me. I stopped near Mister Quinn's chair, fumbling with my bundle of books and lunch. He turned when he saw that nobody was paying attention to him, and he took my hand and drew me toward his desk.

—'This is Tom Paulhan,' he said to the class. 'He comes all the way from Thurman Station, and this is the first day he's ever been to school. I want all of you to say hello.'

—I was ashamed, and I couldn't look up, but I heard them speak, and then I heard some of the girls giggling, and I thought of the sound of the riverwater on the turning pebbles, wishing that I was out in the woods where nobody could stare at me and laugh. It was fun to explore the woods all by myself; it was fun to find things and not tell anybody about them. Instead of wasting my time at school, I could have been lying bellydown on the big rock near the Thurman bridge, watching the baby bass bunting the current; I could have been stalking some twitchnosed chipmunk that stared at me out of the corner of an eye while it sat sideways propped up like a kangaroo; I could have been up at Viele Pond to see the kingfishers diving for chub in the shoals, or, if it were late in the afternoon, to see a deer come from the forest and feed among the lilypads; and even if the bluejays joshed me from the birches once in a while, it wasn't the same as being made fun of by a lot of little boys and girls.

—Mister Quinn said, 'Tom, take that seat next to Aaron. This is his first day here too.'

—I went up the aisle to the desk that Mister Quinn had pointed out, and after putting my things in the cupboard below, I folded my hands and waited for the lesson to begin. I listened for a while, but I didn't understand the words *addition* and *subtraction*, and I looked around to see whether the lesson was as hard for the others as it was for me. The first face I saw was Aaron's. I couldn't tell how long he'd been watching me, but I was tired of being stared at as if my pants were open. This Aaron—there was no expression at all on his face. He just sat there, eyeing me like a little animal, like one of those chipmunks that I trailed in the woods. I tried to make him blink, but he didn't seem to realize what I was doing, and finally I had to turn away.

—When the time came for the geography lesson, Mister Quinn unrolled a map of the United States from the top of the blackboard frame. New York was outlined in red crayon, and the shape of it was something like a shoe with a spiked heel. I found a few other states that reminded me of things I'd seen—Michigan was a mitten, and Florida a cow's tit, and Nebraska a cannon, and Connecticut a meatcleaver—but no matter how hard I tried to twist them with my mind, they just never were *exactly* like the shapes that I knew.

—Aaron raised his hand and said, 'Mister Quinn, please would you show where is Warrensburg on that map?'

—'Warrensburg isn't important enough to be on a map of the United States,' Mister Quinn said. 'Here's Albany, though, and we're only about ninety miles north.'

—'Why isn't Warrensburg important enough?'

—'It's too small.'

—'I don't think it's small," Aaron said, 'How could it be small with all them houses and stores, and the Adirondack Inn, and the paper mill?'

—'It's small compared to a city like Albany.'

—'I don't think it's small," Aaron said.

—Mister Quinn laughed, saying, 'That's because *you're* small. If you'll all come up close here, I'll show you where Warrensburg ought to be.'

—We crowded around him, and he took a pin from his lapel and made a hole in the map about half an inch over Albany. 'You see that little hole there?' he said. 'Well, that's Warrensburg.'

—Nobody did anything for a couple of seconds, and then Aaron spoke up again. 'How can that little hole be Warrensburg?' he said. 'It's only as big as a pinpoint, and you can't stuff people and houses and trees in a thing that size.'

—Mister Quinn didn't laugh, but I did. I don't know why, but I laughed out loud, and then everybody joined in. We made Aaron look like a dunce.

—'I don't think you ought to laugh at Aaron,' Mister Quinn said. 'He's never seen a map before, and he just doesn't know that these little dots only *stand* for the real places. That pinpoint isn't Warrensburg, Aaron, but it shows you where Warrensburg is, where you'd see it if—if you were a hundred miles above the earth in a balloon. You see, Aaron, you couldn't have a map that showed every place as it *really* is because then your map would be the same size as the world. Even New York is a pretty big place, and the only way we can get an idea of every part of it at the same time is by using a map. Do you understand now, Aaron?'

—Aaron stared at the map for a little while longer, and then he said, 'No. I can't see every part of New York on the map; there's only a lot of little dots with words alongside of them. Where's the people and the houses and the animals, and where's all the rivers and hills and woods and fields? I can see them things with my own eyes when I look out of that window, but only a dunce would say they was on that map.'

—Everybody laughed but Mister Quinn—*Aaron* was such a dunce....

❖ ❖ ❖

Platt: ... She said, "He's upwards of seven years old now, and it's high time for him to be getting a little learning."

My father let out such a holler that you'd of thought he sat down in hot fat. "Learning!" he said. "Now, what the hell for?"

That was only the beginning. The argument lasted all summer long, and a nastier dispute this town never seen. Morning, noon, and night they fought it out, and many a time when they was at it hot and heavy, my father laid the flat of his hand alongside my mother's jaw to see if he couldn't stop her nagging him about me being allowed to go to school. Things come to such a pass after a while that I wouldn't of give a damn if they murdered each other so long as they quit making that everlasting stink.

My mother must of been around forty at the time, but what with the way she'd been used since she got married, you'd of figured her to be sixty if she was a day. No God damn iron machine ever had to stand the wear and tear that she did. She wasn't any wife in my father's eyes; she was just a combination cook, hired girl, wet nurse, and whoor; and I seen him working the living spunk out of her at all them trades, by night as well as in the daylight.

I caught him at it by accident the first time. I'd got out of bed to get me a glass of water, and to reach the kitchen I had to pass by the room that my mother and father was sleeping in only that night they didn't happen to be sleeping. The door was half open, and even though there wasn't any lamp burning, I could make out what was going on in there because a throw of moonshine fell right onto the bed.

There was the old bull working away like he meant to plow a furrow clean through the mattress. I didn't know what he was doing to my mother, but I got the feeling that it was something so terrible to her that she couldn't make a sound, and with my father snorting like a hog with its snoot buried in swill, I got the notion that he was torturing something deaf and dumb. I had the feel of his iron in the pit of my stomach; I was underneath of him, and he was tearing me apart.

I forgot all about the glass of water, I forgot about everything in the whole wide world except that long burning gash he'd tore in my belly, and even now, so many years afterwards, I don't know how long I stood there before my guts bucked, and I ran. I ran, and the only place I could run to was my room. I shut the door and bolted it, thinking maybe I could lock out what I just seen, but I couldn't. It was right there next to me in bed, and the bed was shaking with it, and the air was filled with the sound of grunting and snuffling, and close enough for me to of touched it with my hand was that deaf and dumb body—and then I couldn't stand being in bed any more and I got in the closet, and sitting there in a corner, shivering, I remembered that once before I done the selfsame thing, and I tried to think of that other time, and it come back to me very slow, like I was drunk....

... I seen a milksnake coming towards me through the grass, a little finger of a snake colored like cocoa, but I didn't see it with my eyes—I seen it with the bridge of my nose, the hollow in my upper lip, and the crack in my chin; I seen it with my bellybutton and my balls; I seen it with the whole centerline of my body. All at once I ran in the woodshed, grabbed up the hatchet, and rushed back to hunt for the snake, feeling like I'd choke if I didn't find it. I found it, all right, and when I did I went down on my knees in the grass and chopped it to halfinch bits, and I stayed there on my knees even after each little chunk stopped moving, and I minced them to a slowturning mush, and then, taking a last look at the pasty stew,

I ran. I ran up to my room and locked myself in the closet, and I stayed there in the dark till I knew it was dark outside....

...And for the second time I shut the world out, and in the morning I sneaked out of the house without eating, without looking at anybody, afraid that if I seen my father's face I'd pick up a cleaver and bury it in the top of his skull. It was a matter of days before I could bring myself to look at my mother either, and when I finally did I was surprised to find out that there wasn't anything about her to show I didn't dream what I seen my father doing to her that night.

When I think about her now, I always see her in the same dress, a washedout cotton rag, and far's I know it was one of the two she had to her name. She wasn't any beauty—we don't have so many beauties around here—and she wasn't even salty for Warrensburg, but all the same I happened to like the way she looked. Her hair was thin, but what she did have was very fine, and she wore it parted in the middle and brushed down flat on either side so's to make a little braided coil in back of her head. She kept herself neater than an egg, and nobody ever seen the day when she had so much as a hair out of plumb. She had big raw hands, but in a matter like a sprain she could simply work wonders with them, and if you had a headache it wouldn't be ten minutes before she'd have it kneaded out for you with fingers that looked like wood and felt like fur.

She said, "He's upwards of seven years old now, and it's high time for him to be getting a little learning."

He said, "Learning! Now, what the hell for?"

"So's he can know about things that he'll never find out in back of a plow."

"If working in back of a plow is good enough for me, then it's got to be good enough for him. Why should he be getting any benefits that nobody ever give me?"

"Because he's the only son you're ever going to have."

"You don't have to be chucking that in my face all the time."

"Looks like I do. The way you treat an only child, anybody'd think you had a dozen of them, but there's no more where Aaron come from, and you better make up your mind to it right quick. The other five is laying out there in the pasture, and so help me God, there's times I'm glad they was all took away from you."

"And what kind of times is that?"

"Like now. Like when you show you got a heart about as big as a acorn and twice as hard."

"Talk like that don't sit so good on me. I've gave that boy all he's entitled to, and good measure."

She laughed, saying, "Sure you did—with the flat of your hand. You've beat him so black and blue that he couldn't sit, stand, or lay down. You gave him good measure of that, all right, but nothing else."

Them heavy hands of his started in working like he was just itching to try them out on her neck, but he never seen the day he could really throw a scare into her.

She only said, "It's a wonder to me that God don't strike you down dead."

"God strike *me* down! There ain't any God big enough to turn that little trick. You won't get anywheres trying to put a curse onto me. There's plenty of work to be done around this here farm, and I don't see that God damn God of yours helping me out none. I send the boy off to school, and all the thanks I get for it is I have to do his share. I got enough the way it is, and by Jesus, I don't like it worth a shit!"

"Everybody sends a child to school."

"What's the good of schooling for a farmer? He don't get any place studying arithmetic. That don't learn him anything about how to run a farm. Working's the only way you get the hang of that."

"There's plenty of time for working. He's got a whole lifetime of working staring him in the face, and it's the wrong thing for you to be making a slave out of him when he's only a little boy. I say there's plenty of time for him to be breaking his back. Right now he ought to be learning things and taking some ease, because God knows he ain't going to have any soft snap of it when he gets bigger—at least not with you around to gall the life out of him. He's a smart boy, and he learns quick, and who knows but what he just wasn't cut out to be any farmer? ..."

My father slapped her across the face hard enough to start her plates, and them dollar hunks of red rubber bulged out of her mouth like her jawbones come loose. She only put up her hands and pushed the teeth back; she didn't cry. Her mouth was bleeding, but she didn't cry. She went right on arguing like nothing ever happened.

"Maybe he could learn to be something else."

My father was bullmad, and he'd of hit her again if he thought he could of made her shut up. "*What* else?" he said.

"Anything he wants."

"That's just what I'm scared of—him getting a snootful of learning and going off some place so's I don't have anybody to help me with the working of the farm."

"The farm can go to seed for all I care. The boy's entitled to pick and choose the way he wants, and if he don't want to be any farmer, then it's a sin to make him."

"You're calling on that God again," he said. "Didn't I just finish telling you I don't scare at that kind of talk?" And he went out of the house and didn't come back till after we went to bed.

Then one day, out of a clear sky, he give in. He just walked up to my mother and said he'd thought the matter over and changed his mind. She was so dumbstruck that all she could do was stand there and stare at him with her mouth open, and then she started in to cry so terrible that you'd of thought he told her just the opposite to what he did. She grabbed me and took me outside, and she sat down in the grass and hugged me, rocking and rocking me like I was still a little baby, all the time crying because she was so glad.

I remember the first day I went to school. My mother walked with me down to where the farm road hit the Warrensburg pike, and when she stopped she took my face in her hands and looked down at me with her eyes running over, and then all at once she kissed me for the last time I can ever remember, and she hurried back towards the farm without once looking around.

I slung my homemade canvas satchel over my shoulder and started the fourmile downhill climb. Back of Potash Mountain the sun wasn't up yet to take the mist out of the valley, and it was cold in the gray earlymorning, colder than ever where the wind lifted the chill off of some brook in the woods and carried it across the road. It was sixthirty, and I took my time, wondering the whole way down what school was going to be like ....

⚜   ⚜   ⚜

Paulhan talked all night long. He talked in one continuous burst, as if he were reciting a narrative that he was afraid of forgetting, but in the now dissolving darkness, his voice too began to dissolve, losing itself in the cold air like smoke, and at last, failing entirely, it subsided into the vapor drifting from his open mouth. Then it was quiet in the barn, and the only sound to enter the silence was the occasional hissing of oatstraw as one of the horses disturbed its bedding.

Platt stood up, stepped across Paulhan, and went to the window. Leaning against a rotted crib, he peered out at the morning from behind a dusty screen of abandoned cobwebs. The day was clear, the sun blaring off the snow and jumping hollows where shadow was a wash of gray as soft as ash. Paulhan stirred a little, and the straw under him crumbled like crackers. Platt turned, looked at the outstretched form for a few seconds, and then walked out of the stall.

He went back to the house and ate the biggest meal of his life. Hungrier than usual to begin with, he became angry at the sight and smell of food, carnal during the preparing of it, and finally, when it lay before him on the kitchen table, temporarily insane. He assaulted it as if it had suddenly taken the form of everything human that he hated, as if it were the seeing, hearing, smelling, tasting, feeling, composite living shape of all those who had inflicted evil upon him; and he ate as if the cutting and mastication were the killing, and the swallowing the burial, of his enemies.

He knew what he had done. He knew because he spoke his knowledge to the doorknobs, the crockery, the metal canisters, the rubberlipped masonjars; he spoke it to the wearying pattern of the oilcloth that covered the table and shelves, to the worn areas that looked as if they were blurred by pieces of waxed paper; and he spoke it to the mastiff stove, the immobile pots and dishes and pans, the boxes and cans and all the other stockstill objects that hemmed him in. He spoke to these, saying, *"You sonofabitch, you sweet sonofabitch—Amram Platt, my own father!"*

And once more the barn became the core of his consciousness—not the barn, but a stall in the barn; not the stall, but a man lying on the floor of it; and further, not even the man, but his speaking mouth—and toward this center Platt felt himself drawn. He tried to resist, he tried to unfascinate his mind....

⚜ ⚜ ⚜

—... There was the map with its tightfitting colored pieces, its speckle of citydots, its waving riverlines; and there was Mister Quinn with his wooden pointer; and there, surrounding him and the map, were all the children; and as I stood among them, listening to Mister Quinn's voice and watching the tip of the pointer move from place to place, all this and all else fainted from my mind, and for a while there was nothing; and then very slowly a dream began to turn in great but pleasant fatigue, rising slowly, slowly expanding like a balloon, and it swelled up from the bare floor of my brain, and I knew then that there would be a time when the thin membrane of the dream would burst.... And there were years of those days, days and months and years that were not mandivisions of time, but one long continuation that flowed past me like an endless outgoing tide....

❧ ❧ ❧

Platt:... Quinn wasn't any schoolteacher; he was a God damn wizard. He had a bag of tricks that would of beat a magician all hollow, and just being let go to school was the greatest thing that'd happened in all the seven years of my life. Not a day of it did I miss for four solid months, rain or shine, fall or winter, sick or sound.

It was a long walk down to the schoolhouse and a bitch of a climb to get back, but I never give it a second thought. I was doing fine for a beginner, even catching up on the rest of the boys my age, and for a while I didn't take any notice of how my father was piling on the work back to the farm. I done whatever I found waiting for me, never thinking about it, never seeing that more and more was being left over for me every week, never wondering why I was so played out some nights that I couldn't eat my supper, let alone do my lessons.

I didn't smell a rat till the day I got sat up on a stool in a corner of the classroom for falling asleep when Mister Quinn was talking. He'd always been good to me, but that was the third time I corked off on him, and he was out to learn me a lesson that I wouldn't forget. Sitting up there in front of all them snickering little squirts with that God damn clown's hat on my head, I had the whole afternoon to think—and I didn't miss.

When it come to getting his own way, my father was underhanded as a weasel and cuter than a raccoon, and it was a pretty sly little stunt, him making out he didn't have any objections to me going to school, but even so I should of seen the catch to it right at the start because he sung offkey when I got back to the farm the very first day.

He took me aside, saying, "I'm letting you take a little book learning against my best judgment, but your ma wants it like that, so I'm not going to put my foot down. There's something I'd just like you to bear in mind, though, and that's that you still got a certain share of work to do around here, and the first time I catch you shirking it I'm going to whale the living ass off of you. Understand that, you little snotnose?"

I nodded, and he nodded back, and then he turned loose that mean loud laugh of his. "Come on," he said, "and I'll show you your share."

He showed it, all right, he give me so much to do that by suppertime my prat was fair dragging on the ground.

Falling asleep in school was only a starter. Pretty soon I was missing whole days down there, trying to clean up the jobs my father left over for me, and once that begin to come off I was pretty near through. For every day I stayed away from school I had to work twice as hard to catch up on my lessons, and I just never did. I got myself the character of being the biggest dumb ox in school, and day after day the kids poked fun at me, and when I finally couldn't stand it any more, I grabbed ahold of the one that was egging the others on—his name was Tom Paulhan—and I buried his front teeth in his lips.

Mister Quinn couldn't see that for dust, and he sent me up the hill to think it over for a couple of weeks, and that cost me my last hope of going in the advance at the middle of the year. It didn't help me any to get left back, and the kids shamed me out worse than ever, and then even Mister Quinn begin thinking I didn't have any business being in school. He turned up at the farm one afternoon and told my mother I was just wasting my time; he said I didn't seem to have any head for a scholar, and I was holding up the rest of the class, and maybe it'd be a good idea if I bowed out.

That kind of talk took all the heart out of my mother. She knew what was keeping me down to the foot of the class, only she was too ashamed of my father to tell Mister Quinn about it. All she could do was beg him to give me another chance, promising she'd see to it that I done better work in the future, and finally he give in.

That night she went to work on my father to get him to ease up on me, but he raised such a stink that you could of heard him clean down to Lake George.

"Christ Almighty!" he said. "Am I supposed to do *all* the work around here? Didn't I give in to your foolishness and send the boy off to school when you ast me to? What more do you want? Maybe I should let the farm go to pot just so's the little pisscutter can get himself educated! Well, you got another think coming if you expect any such a thing. It's just too damn bad he can't make out down there to school, but that's his funeral, not mine. He'll do his share of the work, or else I'll break his ass for him. Nobody makes me the laughingstock of Warrensburg account of any sevenyearold bastard!"

The upshot was I had to get along as best I could, and maybe I'd of done all right if things didn't get even harder than they was. When my father seen I was still able to crawl off down the hill in the mornings, he put the screws on for fair. Every day he bobbed up with something he called extraspecial that just had to be cared for right away, and pretty soon, with all them extraspecial things, I was staying home about as much as I was going to school—but by that time I didn't care any more. I was sick and tired of sitting around in school with a bunch of kids that knew so much more than me; and with Mister Quinn just leaving me rot there on my prat week after week and never calling on me even once, I got to thinking that maybe I'd of been a lot better off if he didn't listen to my mother about giving me another chance.

I got fed up one day, and when I come back to the farm I told my father I was done with school for good and all, and then

I took my books and chucked them through the privyhole. My father clapped me on the back, saying he sure was glad to see me doing the sensible thing. The feel of his hand on me was as bad as taking a header in the stone boat along with the books. I shook him off, shivering like you do when your fingernail scratches on slate, and he got sore.

"What's a matter, you little devil?" he said. "Too good for folks now you got some learning into you? Maybe this'll show you some respect." And he placed one next to my ear that come close to tearing my head off.

I picked myself up and backed away, saying, "You sonofa-bitch—you sweet sonofabitch, you!"

He galloped at me like a locomotive, but I put plenty of day-light in between us, and then I turned around and hollered back at him, "You're a sonofabitch, a lousy old sonofabitch!"

He come mighty near to having a stroke then and there. If he'd of caught me, he'd of killed me on the spot, but I knew bet-ter than to let him get them hooks into me at a time like that, so all day I kept to the woods above the farm, and when it was dark I sneaked back to the barn, let myself in, and fell asleep in that same stall where I found Paulhan.

That's where I was when my father nabbed me in the morn-ing. I was still dopey with sleep and weak from going so long without food, but I remember that my mother was right in back of him when he come in and tore me out of the hay. She tried to come between us, but all she got for her pains was a shove that sent her flying to hell out of the stall. Then my father give me what he called a lesson.

He beat me till he got tired, that's all. Time and again my mother tried to pull me away from him, but nothing in Christ's world could of stopped that bull once he got started, nothing except his arms got so weary that he couldn't hardly lift them up any more. By that time I didn't know what was happening. I found out later that there wasn't a white spot left onto my body, and all the week I was laid up in bed I couldn't budge so much as a finger without feeling like I was falling apart.

That was only a lesson he give me, you understand, but don't ast what he was trying to learn me. If he thought he was going to benefit by it, he must of been touched. He only made me hate him worse than ever. I hated him pretty bad before that beating, but afterwards I couldn't stand the sight of him. I couldn't stay in the same room where he was, or eat at the same table, because just knowing he was there was enough to addle my guts, and the sound of his voice made me think of knives, long sharp knives, and hayforks with tines honed down like needles, and axes with blades as thin as paper, and the smell of him reminded me of blood, and my eyes would fix on anything that shined like steel, anything that had a cutting edge to it, and sometimes I'd find myself moving towards that shining thing, sometimes actually holding it in my hands—and then I'd have to run away.

I hated him so hard, and that beating took so much out of me, that I finally come down with a fever. My father wouldn't call the doctor, though, because he figured I was only making out I was sick so's I wouldn't have to work, but my mother could read the signs, and she knew damn well I wasn't playacting. She done her best to wheedle my father into getting Doc Slocum up from Warrensburg, but he promised her trouble if she didn't let up on him. She'd lost five before me, and she wasn't going to let the sixth and last die right under her eyes even if my father went and busted every bone in her body, so after he fell asleep one night she sneaked out of the house and tramped all the way down to the village for Slocum.

When Slocum looked me over, he got so cold mad that he damn near jumped out of his britches: I had typhoid, and if my mother'd waited any longer to call him I'd of been deader than a side of pork. Even so, he had his work cut out for him, and the only time he went off of the farm in the next three days was to get some medicine from his office. It was touch and go whether I'd stiffen out on him, but finally he brung me around.

My mother told me afterwards that he made it his business to tell my father what he thought of him. Just before he went away he cornered the old man and blacknamed him up, down, and across for being the hardest bastard he'd turned up in twenty years of doctoring the county.

My father took it without a word. He waited for Slocum to get done, and then he pulled some money out of his pocket, saying, "How much I owe you, Doc?"

"You know what you can do with it, don't you?" Slocum said.

"Sure—ram it."

"Well, what're you waiting for?"

"For you to get the hell off of my farm."

It was weeks and weeks before I could creep out to some sunny spot in the woods, and all afternoon I'd lay there in the pineneedles baking in the heat, sometimes drowsing off for hours on end, sometimes just looking up at the sky and watching the clouds foam away like soapsuds, but always I'd lay so still that the birds and animals took me for part of the forest, and they went about their little business without ever knowing they was being spied on, without being afraid.

That was the one real vacation I had in my life. Slocum must of throwed a scare into my father with that dressing down because for once he let up on me. The Doc probably told him there wasn't any rushing the kind of a sickness I had unless he wanted to see me dead—and if I went and died on him he'd of been pretty near as broke up as if he lost one of his horses. That's the only reason why he give me a while to rest up—because I wouldn't of been worth a nickel to him under a headstone.

There's some people that you just take one swift look at, just get a whiff of from far off, and you have to say that there's a man ought to be dead. Amram Platt, my own father, was such a man. He didn't have the respect of anybody in the world. His own wife used to call on God to strike him down with a bolt of lightning, and many a time I'd wonder how any woman could of carted him around in her belly for nine solid months; you'd think she'd of rotted away.

The Reverend Mister Titus down here preaches a lot of wind about you should honor your father, but he'd sing a different tune if he had the one that I did. In a man's lifetime he comes across a lot of things he can't figure out any reason for except maybe to make him more miserable than he ought to be—lice, rats, flies, and a whole assortment of flying and crawling creatures—but every one of them's a blessing alongside of my father. You swat flies, and you trap rats, and you stick a hayfork in snakes, but what in God's world are you supposed to do with a *man*—a man that you know way down deep in your heart is a damn sight lower than vermin?

The law's all wrong that says an eye for an eye, and a tooth for a tooth. The way I see it is, vermin's vermin whether it creeps on its belly, or flies in the air, or walks around in pants....

❧   ❧   ❧

Platt went out into the day, the sudden furnace of the snow stunning his eyes like smoke. All morning the sky had been swept by the wind, and now there remained only a few shallow smears of gray watercolor to fog the wedgwood ceiling. Gyroscopes of snow spun on the flats, their fine camphorations veering into Platt's face and douching it like spray from an atomizer.

The sloping drifts slid out from under him as he went down to the brook. A conduit of ice had formed above the fastmoving run, but here and there it had caved in, and the water chuckled through the broken vault, turning over and over as it fell away downhill and churned itself to a pebblesounding simmer. For a long time Platt stood there, listening to the water and resting his eyes on the gray shadow his body cast across the glittering crease in the snow.

For two days a thought had been burgeoning in his brain, and although he had tried to stifle his awareness of its growth, he could no longer deny the knowledge, and with the relaxing of effort the thought at once came violently to flower. Clenched before, held compact by his positive will, it opened now like a fist, and it groped for the remotest reaches of his mind, invaded all the storehouses of his memory, tore down the partition that had been concealing the one purpose of his life; and he knew irrevocably, within earshot of the distant mirth of the little brook, that if he did nothing, if he merely allowed time to pass him as the brookwater was passing him, his single purpose would be accomplished....

❧ ❧ ❧

—...All afternoon I lay on the floor watching the world come toward me, the telegraph poles, the dipping wires, the pyramids of ballast, the racks of rails, and beyond the right of way the broad sunbright plain that burned like a great low gas-flame under the rug of lupine that covered it as far as the curve of the earth. All afternoon this platform of flowers moved past my face, but the mountains beyond, more immobile than the sky, remained where they were. All afternoon the freight had been tortured toward them, and still they loomed like an arrested wave in the now purpling distance, clearer now because the sun was behind them, yet far away and unapproachable.

—The long haul made a long slow bend, and I saw a mile ahead of me to the team of moguls that draped their twin rolling manes over the rocking boxcars. The train slowed down to enter a siding, barely making headway as the trucks tumbled over the frogs, and then, drifting until the brakeshoes were clamped against the tires, the accordion of cars collapsed to a halt. Two lavender braids of smoke drilled high into the motionless air. It was very quiet.

—And I thought: *I want this—I want only to know that I shall hear no voices, that I shall see no movement, that I shall fear no invasion of my mobile space in the void. Cut me off from the long tradition of trespass. Dismiss me from history....*

—The leading mallet barked twice, and diminished by distance, the sound trembled back over the cars, ricocheted, and fled away over the groundwaves. Reversed to shake out the slack, the engines drove their mileaway iron thunder through the couplings all the way to the caboose. Deep and long, twice again they bayed in the dark, and the train was rolling. The wheels began to pound the notches in the rails, slowly at first, but with slowly increasing speed, and I settled myself against a wall of the empty, waiting for the quarantine of the rising rhythm.

—The door shrieked on its rusted rollers, and in the widened oblong of navyblue night bobbed the head and shoulders of a man. The form sprang at the opening and sprawled on the floor of the car, and for a moment it lay there, dummystill but trespassing, and then, in the dim faraway flare of an opened firebox, the form grew animate again, sat up, and searched the gloomy grottoes of the boxcar. Just as the head swiveled toward my corner the flare died, and there was darkness again, deeper than before.

—Over the mechano of rolling wheels, I heard nothing. Except for the wedge of vision between me and the open door, the car was darker than the outside night, and I was alone with the invisible intruding stranger. For a long time I sat still, wondering where the man was, whether he was in front of me now or to one side of me, whether he was standing up, sitting down, or lying flat on the splintery planking; and I wondered too what the man looked like, whether he was young or old, big or little, white or black. For a long time I sat still, not daring to move.

—Then a match made its quick firecracker sneeze, and my michelin shadow came to life in a corner of the empty, quivering like a waterimage with the quivering of the hand that held the match. The man was off to my right, and I turned, but he flipped the light away before I had a chance to see his face, and once more I waited in the darkness.

—I didn't hear him come over to me: I smelled him. Through the evidence of countless cargoes, through the indelible stain of odors that tattooed the woodwork of the car—cinnamon, smoked meat, mahogany, and mold; calico, mildew, verdigris, and rust; coffee, cork, burlap, and benzine; the brine of barreled fish, the acid of newsprint, the putty of painted iron, the rainwater of damp lumber, the vinegar ghost of transient wine—through all these came the odor of the invading stranger, and it wiped them out as a fog wipes out a forest. It was a prison odor that embalmed him, an odor distilled from urine, musk, phlegm, sweat, melting teeth, and carbolic; it was an odor of disinfected decay, flavored by the ferment of a thousand rancid meals—a prison odor!—and then his hand found my thigh, pressed it, and sidled toward my groin.

—I tore away from him, from his odor of laundered confinement, and I stood up and ran toward the open door to breathe the clarity of the unconfined night. He came after me, touched me again, fumbled with my body—and the prison odor came with him. I shoved him, and he went backward on his heels, and at that instant the car rocked into a bend, tearing his feet out from under him as if he'd been standing on a rug. He made a long flat dive through the door, and I didn't hear the sound his body made when it hit the ballast, spun like an eddy, and rolled down the embankment.

—And I thought: *I want this—I want only to know that I shall hear no voices, that I shall see no movement, that I shall fear no invasion of my mobile space in the void. Cut me off from the long tradition of trespass. Dismiss me from history....*

✤ ✤ ✤

Platt: ... He come out to the woodshed, and he said, "Your ma just went and died. I'm going to take me down to Warrensburg and get the undertaker. Be back in twothree hours."

Then he started for the barn, stopping on the way to fill his pipe and light it—and all the while I stood where I was, holding the axe in my hands and looking at the creases in the back of his neck. And I remember that I stood there running my thumb over the nicks in the blade till long after he'd hitched the horse to the buggy and drove off down the road.

He'd left her where she fell—on the floor of the kitchen—and I stopped in the doorway for a little while, watching a fly crawl up her face towards some sweat that was still shining on her forehead, and it come to me all of a sudden the things you hear people say about the dead, how they always look younger than when they was alive, and how they look rested and peaceful like they was only taking a nap and having a good dream.

My mother was the first dead human being I ever set eyes on, and she didn't look like she was sleeping there with her face in the ashes alongside of the stove. She looked dead, worse than dead—she looked killed. All over her, sunk in like heelprints in mud, was the story of the grief she'd had ever since she got married, the worries, the hard work, the sourness of being disappointed again and again for years.

I carried her in the parlor and laid her out on the sofa. Then I got a towel and a basin of water, and I washed her face and hands, and I combed her hair too, but even so she made such a distressing sight that I hated to look at her. It was like paying a call on somebody that wasn't expecting you, and you found them looking so poorly that you felt like you was spying on them.

While I sat there waiting, I tried to remember a time when she'd looked different, when there'd been some life in her, when she didn't make me think I'd roused her up in the middle of the night—and the only time I could call to mind was when she told me about a journey she'd made when she was a little girl: her father'd took her to Albany! That little ninetymile trip was just about the most wonderful thing she'd done in all her days, and if she told me about it once, she told me a hundred times over. I heard it the first time when I was fourfive years old, and I heard it the last only a month or so before she died, and in them ten years a crumby fourday outing changed to a voyage around the world. At the start the story was always pretty much the same, but little by little it grew in her mind till finally she was telling me about things that couldn't of happened to her nor anybody else on the face of the globe. It was the one and only scrap of enjoyment that she could remember, though, and I never had the heart to spoil it.

She was buried the next day. About a dozen people drove up from Warrensburg, most of them Boltons, but only the Reverend Mister Titus come in the house; all the rest stayed out on the porch near a window and listened to him preach his little piece about exactly who was going to inherit the earth and how God always seen to it that the righteous was rewarded in heaven.

He must of went on like that for half an hour before my father butted in and told him he'd gargled enough hogwash to win my mother's reward hands down. All them Boltons out on the porch stared at him like dead mackerel, and Mister Titus looked mighty grieved about being hurried along just when he was getting the snot cleared out of his windpipe, but for once I had to side with my father. All that trash about God taking care of the meek and lowly was beginning to set pretty heavy on my guts too. They inherited the earth, all right, but what Mister Titus declined to say was just how much of it. They got a neat little parcel big enough to fit a coffin in, and if they was fools for luck they got a threedollar headstone to go over it. Sure they inherited the earth—worms and all.

When Titus turned off the gas, six of us picked up the coffin and carried it up the hill to the grave I dug the day before at the edge of the woods. The others followed along in back of us, and after Titus done a little more armwaving we let the box down in the hole. Some of the men wanted to help me fill in the dirt, but I told them I'd do it myself, and then the whole crowd, even my father, went off down the hill again, and I was left up there alone.

There was something so cheap about the way my mother lived and died. I picked up the spade ....

⚜ ⚜ ⚜

—... It was late afternoon. Over a crack made by a pair of longdipping ridges on the far side of the Pond, a thunderhead boomed up like an enormous fungoid, and from the crowd of trees behind the little dock now and then broke the sound of leaf-dancing, sometimes far away and no more audible than the folds of a silk garment rubbing, sometimes spreading toward me from tree to tree as if there were many garments in procession.

—I sat on the dock, staring at the moving but unbroken water, in which clouds trembled like poached eggs. Darningneedles scaled through the air, stopping dead sometimes and beating their mica wings so rapidly that only their burntmatch bodies were visible. Among the reeds near the bank, bullfrogs gulped a sprungrhythm chorus, and in the celerystalks of a birch overhanging the water, a red squirrel creaked like a stiff hinge.

—For a long time these were the only sounds, and then, muffled by the forest, came the distant explosions of a laboring motor. The car stopped at the lodge, and after a few moments I saw Nate coming down the path leading to the Pond. In one hand he carried a bass rod, and in the other a baitcan made of galvanized iron. He lowered the can into the shallows, and then he sat down on one of the dockpiles to thread his line through the agates.

—'Seen Harry Reoux last week,' he said. 'He told me about you being back.'

—Nate hadn't changed; the only thing different about him was the way he dressed. He wore a chauffeur's uniform of dark green whipcord; his cap was made of the same material, and on the black linoleum visor, stamped in gold within a golden lavalière of pines, were the words *Thoreau's Walden—A Camp For Moderns.*

—'Nice rig you're wearing,' I said.

—'Kind of pretty, ain't it?' he said, taking off the cap and turning it over in his hands.

—'It certainly is, especially that cap. Put it on again, will you, Nate?'

He raised the cap and was about to put it on his head when he happened to look at my face. Disgusted, he pitched the cap off into the brush.

—'That's no way to treat a good cap,' I said.

—'I'm sick of it. Everybody kids me.'

—'They're jealous, that's all.'

—'Jealous nothing. They're laughing their heads off, and so are you. If I'd of knew I was going to get togged out like the village idiot, I'd never of took the job.'

—'When'd you get it, Nate?'

—'Twothree weeks ago. The old man made me grab it when it come along. I'm supposed to stick it out all summer, but the way I feel now I'm going to run the bus right smack in a ditch one of these days. I'd sooner go fishing any time.'

—'The bass are pretty good right now,' I said, 'but they're beginning to lay off the frogs.'

—'They're always good this time of year, and I been missing out on all the fun, but job or no job, I'm going to flip a few minnies at them weeds this afternoon.'

—'How many'd you bring?' I said.

—'Thirtyodd, and all beauts. One in particular, he's in that can fighting like a trout. He's King of the Minnies, and I want you should use him.'

—'Thanks, Nate. How about changing the water?'

—'Don't have to. I done that down to Bennett's pipe.'

—'Let's get started, then,' I said.

—I went up to the lodge for one of the rods that Harry Reoux had lent me, and then Nate and I got into the scow and shoved off. I rowed out toward a float of weeds at the south end of the Pond, and when we were near it Nate made the first cast. He had a quick strike, but the bass he brought in was so small that he threw it back without bothering to measure it.

—Then he fished around in the baitcan for what he'd called the King of the Minnies, and he handed it to me. I hooked it upward through the lips and stripped several yards of line from my reel while Nate brought the boat broadside to the weeds and rowed gently along the open water. Standing up in the stern, I slung the minnow toward the grass. It fell quietly and darted for the roots, but I checked it. The water was about four feet deep, and against the light brown bottom the little chub stood out clearly even though it was a couple of boat-lengths away.

—Suddenly the bait vanished. The line that I'd stripped began to slide through my fingers, and I was about to strike when I heard Nate talking.

—'Don't be stingy,' he said. 'Let him have it for a while. Give him all the line he wants.'

—I stripped more line, and again it went out through the guides. The tip of the rod jigged like a loose wire.

—'Give him more,' Nate said. 'If he still wants line, he's only got the tail in his mouth. Strip it again.'

—By that time I'd played out nearly twenty yards of line. Letting the bass have another five, I dragged the reel. The rod gave, but not the line, and very quickly I made a short hard strike, up and sideways. The rod bent like tinfoil as the line cut out of the water toward the weeds. Then it wilted and fell to the surface.

—'Take up that slack!' Nate shouted. 'Take it up fast, or you lose him!'

—I thought I'd already lost him, but I tore the slack in anyway. About ten feet of it came through the agates, and the rod drooped.

—'You're boss now,' Nate said. 'Play him careful, and keep his nose away from them weeds.'

—In open water, the fight lasted about ten minutes, the bass breaking five times, the last time only a few feet from the gunwale of the scow. Then it bored to the bottom and sulked in the mud. I had to put the rod down and haul in the line hand over hand. Nate used the net for me.

—'A sweet one,' Nate said. 'I bet he runs over two pound. You'd not of caught him if you didn't listen to me and use that King of the Minnies.'

—We took turns at casting until long after the sun had gone down, and between us we boated seven bass, Nate taking the largest as he was reeling in his final cast. Thunderheads had come and disappeared, and now one more enormous than any of the others was exploding upward for miles, like the smoke of a burning oilwell.

When we reached the lodge, I asked Nate to wait for me on the porch. I went into the kitchen, took a pot of coffee from the warm oven, and set it among the coals for a few moments. Then I filled two cups and carried them outside.

—'Much obliged, Tom,' Nate said. 'You couldn't think of anything I'd of sooner had than coffee.'

—I sat down in a rocker near the edge of the porch and looked away among the dark trees. Deep in the woods a thrush played its woodwind call, and after an interval another thrush sent back a reply like an echo.

—'I never seen a place I liked better than this,' Nate said. 'I could stay up here all the time. Harry's got just about everything a man'd need right here on the property.'

—'Everything?'

—'Sure. What's missing? He's got as tight a little house as you'll find anywheres in these woods, and he's got a fishpond loaded up to the banks with bass. That's everything. What more could a man ask for?'

—'Oh, I don't know,' I said. 'I like to keep on the move. I get restless once in a while.'

—'I go fishing when I feel like that.'

—'How about some more coffee, Nate?'

—'Some other time. I got to be getting back to *Thoreau's Walden—A Camp For Moderns.*'

—'What do they mean by *modern?*' I said.

—'Hard to say. Might have something to do with the girls running around in them Dutch drawers all the time.'

—'Dutch drawers? You mean bloomers, don't you?'

—'Bloomers or drawers, it don't make no neverminds to me. They don't hardly ever wear dresses—that's all I know.'

—'How about visitors?'

—'Come one, come all, I guess. Well, I'm moving.'

—After Nate had gone, I stayed on the porch for a while. Again I heard a wind approach through the trees, and again I was reminded of a pageant of many silken garments. I thought of *Thoreau's Walden.* I went into the house and looked about idly for a moment or two. Then, turning down the wick of the kerosene lamp, I breathed against the pillar of heat rising from the chimney. The flame wavered and collapsed, and in the darkness I watched a spark race around the rim of the wick and disappear.

—From the Pond to Warrensburg it was a sixmile run over a road so narrow and uneven that it was always unfamiliar at night. I knew where all the overhanging branches were, but I was always startled when the windshield struck them and sprayed itself with moisture thrashed from the leaves. Just beyond the Pond I came upon a rabbit that sat in the lampline like a wooden decoy until the car was almost on top of it, and then it bounded away into the forest. I little further on, a pair of raccoons froze in the road and didn't budge even when I brought the car to a stop five yards away from them. They stood there staring at the trembling onesided moons, and I saw the masks covering their triangular faces, the black bands on their rigid brushes. When I sounded the horn, they moved slowly off, but outside the lightcones they stopped for a moment in final curiosity, now revealing of their presence only four little circles of colored glass.

—*Thoreau's Walden* was seven miles above Warrensburg, on the Montreal pike. Over the entrance to the grounds a large signboard bore the same legend and the same garland of pines that decorated the visor of Nate's cap. After twisting through the woods for about a mile, the driveway ended in a circular enclosure where many cars were parked. When I turned off my motor, I heard the tinsound of distant music coming faintly through the trees. The joints of a spine of light jiggled on the surface of a lake that bordered the enclosure, and tracing the music, I followed a footpath along the waterfront.

—I stopped in the doorway of the dancehall, watching couples bob past me like the wooden animals of a carousel. Dozens of girls skated by, the slatting sleeves of their voluminous shirtwaists now and then revealing the moist halfmoons that hung in their armpits. And with the girls were their interchangeable partners—men like a tray of toys in their moccasins, bright woolen socks, lumberjacks, and corduroys. All of them carried nickel flashlights in their hip pockets.

—Someone tapped me on the shoulder. 'So you couldn't stay away,' Nate said.

—'I came up to see the Dutch drawers,'

—'Like them?'

—'I just got here. How about an introduction to start me off?'

—'You don't need me,' Nate said. 'Just pick out the one you fancy, and if she don't happen to have her heart set on nobody else, maybe she'll take a turn with you—and then again, maybe she won't.'

—I saw a very pretty girl standing behind the stagline. She was a blonde, and her pallor was heightened by the color of her shirtwaist, a deep eveningblue. This was cut sailor fashion; a square collar, on which an eagle was embroidered within a circle of stars, rose over her shoulders and then dropped across her chest to form the lapels of an acute V. The man with her was dressed in the usual outfit; he was smoking a new corncob, and from the regulation pocket of his pants protruded the reflector of an electric torch.

—I asked the girl for a dance, and without saying a word to her companion, she put her arm on my shoulder and danced with me through a break in the stagline. I found that there was no material under the collar of her waist, and although I had a minor shock when my hand touched her back, I didn't take it away. The girl gave no sign of being aware of the contact.

—'What's your name?' she said.

—'Paulhan.'

—'That your first name?'

—'No.'

—'You don't tell your last name up here.'

—'Why not?'

—'You just don't.'

—'Tom, then,' I said. 'What's yours?'

—'Rose.'

—'Why don't you people tell your last names?'

—'What for?' she said. 'You just come up from the city?'

—'No. What makes you think so?'

—'Your getup.'

—'What's the matter with it?'

—'Nothing,' she said, 'only nobody dresses like that up at *Thoreau's Walden*, so I guessed you were one of the ones that came up on the afternoon train. Where you from?'

—'A place near Warrensburg—Viele Pond.'

—'Spell it.'

—'V-i-e-l-e.'

—'What's it mean?'

—'I don't know.'

—'Sounds Indian.'

—'Maybe it is,' I said. 'More likely, though, it's the name of the first white man that owned the property.'

—'It belong to you now?'

—'No. The owner's a man named Harry Reoux.'

—'You stay up there all year round?'

—'I don't stay anywhere all year round.'

—'I come from Perth Amboy. It's only a little ways out of New York, but it's dead like a farm.'

—'A farm isn't dead—it's quiet, that's all. A thing doesn't have to bellow to show you it's alive.' Remembering the conversation I'd had with Nate at the Pond earlier in the evening, I couldn't understand why I'd said this to the girl. Suddenly I began to laugh.

—'What's a joke?' she said.

—'I was just laughing.'

—'You must be pretty dumb to laugh at nothing. When I laugh I got a good reason, and I'm laughing right now because you're just about the rottenest dancer I ever laid eyes on. If I didn't have a sense of humor, I'd leave you flat in the middle of the floor. Take me outside and buy me an icecream cone.'

—On the lawn behind the hall, a crowd was attacking a small booth and shouting for drinks, cigarettes, cones, and candy. Rose put her hand into my pocket and helped herself to some coins.

—'I better go,' she said as she started to make her way through the crowd. 'You'd probably get lost. What kind you want?'

—'A blue one, like your waist.'

—The icecream was melting when Rose came back with it. We crossed the lawn, lapping the mush that oozed over the brims of the cones. I became annoyed with mine and threw it away, but Rose ate the last bit of her double strawberry and then licked the drippings from her fingers.

—'Want to go out on the lake?' she said.

—'I don't care.'

—'Well, make up your mind. I can get somebody else just by whistling.'

—'Can you whistle?'

—'With the best of them.'

—'Let's hear you.'

—She went through the refrain of a popular song. 'How you like it?' she said when she was finished.

—'It was pretty good—but nobody came.'

—'What do you mean—nobody came?'

—'You said you could get somebody else to take you out on the lake just by whistling.'

—'You're a fresh guy.'

—I laughed. 'Come on,' I said, putting my arm around her shoulders.

—On the way to the boathouse, Rose stopped at her cabin for a coat. The outside of the shack was trimmed with slabs of birch from which, here and there, postcards of bark had been peeled. When Rose turned on the electric light, I saw that the inner walls were decorated with a green and blue design of pine trees silhouetted against an evening sky. I was surrounded by sunsets. On one wall four suns were disappearing behind four identical ridges; on another they were going down behind a washstand and a threequarter bed with a box spring.

—'Are all the bunks lighted by electricity?' I said.

—'Sure,' Rose said, 'and they all have running water too. Next year there's going to be a telephone in every cabin. That's what the management said today when we were having lunch.'

—There were several canoes and rowboats. We took a canoe, and I shoved it away from the float with a paddle. Rose lay facing me, supported by a number of small cushions. She asked me for a cigarette and smoked it while I paddled away from the shore.

—After a time she said, 'What kind of a place you got up there at—what's the name of it?'

—'Viele Pond,' I said. 'It's an old hunting lodge owned by some people in Warrensburg.' The canoe moved so quietly through the calm water that I could hear the diminishing music of drops falling from the lifted paddle. 'And what about you, Rose? What do you do for a living? Where do you work?'

—'In a lawyer's office in Newark. I go up there every day from Perth Amboy. I'm a stenographer.'

—'What made you come to *Thoreau's Walden?*'

—'Every summer I get two weeks off with pay and an extra week without if I feel like taking it. I used to go to Atlantic Highlands or Asbury Park on my vacations, but after something that happened last summer I swore off the seashore for good. This year I talked over my plans with Shirley Lukats—that's one of the girls in my office—and she said I should go on one of those cruises to Newfoundland, but just then who should come in but Nonie Tobias? Nonie's my best friend even though we both got different religions. She took a look at Shirley and me, and then she said, "What's the argument about?" I said there wasn't any argument, only I was having a hard time making up my mind where I should go on my vacation. I said, "Here it is only a couple of weeks off, and I can't think of a thing, but this much you can bank on, Nonie—no more seashore for mine." Then Shirley said, "What's a matter with that cruise idea? New*found*land is a country you never been to." Then Nonie said, "My God, Rose, don't tell me Shirley said you should go on a cruise! Why, you wouldn't meet a soul on those boats! They're only for fellows that're out for something free of charge. You take my advice and find yourself a lively little place in the Catskills or the Adirandacks. First of all, you'll have a better time, and second of all, remember no decent fellow goes on a cruise. They're all a lot of drunken bums on those boats." That's what Nonie told me, but even before I made up my mind I was all through with the seashore. It was on account of a book I read for school. I go to nightschool, you know—three times a week. In the English course we had to read a book called *Green Mansions*. I forgot the name of the man that wrote it.'

—I said, 'It's by Hudson.' I wanted to stop myself, but the desire was too feeble, and I added, 'Hendrik Hudson.'

—'That's the man!' Rose said. 'How'd you know?'

—'When I haven't anything better to do, I read a book to kill time. I came across *Green Mansions* in a drugstore. It's a nice story, isn't it? It tells about the woods.'

—'And hasn't it got a queer title?' Rose said. '*Green Mansions!* At first I couldn't understand what it meant, but after I got a couple of chapters into the book, I saw it had something to do with nature. You live in the woods, so that's your mansion, and the woods are green, so the place you live in is a green mansion. When I finished that book, I knew there wasn't going to be any more boardwalks and saltwater taffy as far as I was concerned.'

—'Do you think it different up here in the mountains?'

—'Different!' Rose said. 'Why, it's like night and day! The seashore isn't really *country*. When you come right down to it, what're they got there? A lot of people all dressed up in city clothes riding on the boardwalk in a wheelchair. Even if they wanted, they couldn't do anything but go swimming all day and dancing all night. Day after day, it's the same thing all over again—swimming and dancing, dancing and swimming. There's no woods to go tramping around in, there's no grass to lay down on when you want to look up at the clouds—there's nothing but sand, and then more sand. That isn't my idea of *country* any more. Up here in the mountains, the *feeling* you get when you go out in the open air under skies just as blue as blue! I don't know how to put it, but it *does* something to me; it *gets* me. I always liked nature anyway. Maybe I wouldn't like it all the time, but for a change with Perth

Amboy you'd have a hard time trying to find something better than getting out in the open with ground under your feet—*real* ground, not sand and boardwalks. I'm sure glad I read that book. It changed me a lot—no, not changed, exactly. I always liked nature, remember. Anyhow, the book made me open my eyes.'

—'Are you satisfied with *Thoreau's Walden?*'

—'It's simply perfect. It's just what I was looking for.'

—'When will your vacation be over?'

—'I'm in the middle of my second week. After that, I go back to Perth Amboy unless I decide to take that extra week I was telling you about.'

—Then she asked me about the Viele Pond lodge.

—I said, 'The place is fixed up with furniture that came from Grand Rapids originally, I suppose, but that was so long ago that the stuff is all worn down now to just chairs, tables, and beds. I heat the house with woodstoves; there's a large one in the kitchen and a small one in the parlor. It takes about half an hour to get a good hot woodfire going, and even then it warms you on only one side—but all you have to do is turn about when your back starts to freeze.'

—Rose said, 'It must be a lot colder there than at *Thoreau's Walden.*'

—'It is,' I said. 'The Pond's more than a thousand feet higher than this place. I remember one night early in the summer. I covered myself with everything I could pile on the bed, I wore all my outdoor clothes, and I rolled myself up in three yards of carpet and a piece of sailcloth, but still the cold came through as if I were lying there naked.'

—'Say, that must of been pretty cold!' Rose said.

—I tried to see her face in the darkness. 'Yes,' I said, 'it was pretty cold.'

—'Who does your cooking?'

—'I do it myself.'

—'What do you eat?'

—'The Pond's full of bass, and sometimes for a special treat I try the brooks for trout.'

—'Only fish?'

—'I can make all the trimmings too, even coffee, and that's always the hardest of all.'

—'I know how to make fudge,' Rose said.

—I laughed, the sound getting out of control almost at once.

—'Everything strikes you funny,' Rose said. 'What's a matter now? Don't you like fudge?'

—'Fudge! Why, I'm crazy about it!'

—'Then what's the idea of laughing?—Oh, yes, I knew there was something I wanted to ask you. You was only talking about fish before. How about meat?'

—'Why do you ask so many questions?'

—'I was just wondering.'

—'What makes you think of meat in the middle of the night?'

—'Well, we happened to be talking about food, didn't we?'

—'The girl in that book you say you like so much, the girl in *Green Mansions*—do you think she'd be pestering me about whether I eat meat?'

—'I'm sorry you feel that way about it,' Rose said. 'After all, it *is* pretty romantic out here, isn't it?'

—The canoe drifted in a slight wind that chipped the surface of the lake, and in the silence and darkness I forgot the gaudy shirtwaists of *Thoreau's Walden*, its temporary mountaineers and their storagebattery illumination, and I forgot too the sham discomfort of the log cabins, the wearying presence of suns that would never set. Rose herself was a presence, an invisible one; she had dwindled in my mind until I thought of her as nothing more than an ear at the other end of a telephone connection.

—'The Pond is small, but very beautiful,' I said. 'When I want to swim, I row out to the middle and dive from the boat. I do that because the waterlilies make such a jungle along the banks that I'd never get back to the surface once I'd gone below the pads. I hate the slime on lilystems, and I hate the rough brown cylinders of the cat tail—I hate them, but I want them to be there. I want nothing changed at the Pond. I don't want the forest made over into a playground, for I'm not one of those that run barefooted through it and stop here and there, in loud and public emotion, to embrace the tough flesh of an oak. Early in the morning, under its quilt of slowly turning mist, the Pond looks like zinc. The mist condenses all sound except the blurt of bullfrogs, and even that's unusually faint, as if the mist had changed to wadding in the mouths of the frogs. And sometimes in the late afternoon, if I've been very quiet during the day, a deer comes out of the woods and feeds on the lilies at the edge of the Pond.'

—'I'm sorry I talked about meat,' Rose said....

—A couple of days after the dance, I drove down to Warrensburg for my mail. There was only one letter, and it was from Rose. She wrote:

Dear Tom,

Can I call you Tom, or am I presuming on our short friendship? Kindly notice I say friendship and not acquaintanceship. We had such a marvelous time the other night, watching the sun rise and everything—you remember, Tommy?—that I feel as if I know you for a very long time. And when two people know each other for a very long time, they are friends.

Well, here it is two days before the end of my vacation, and what am I to do? Ever since we parted I have been ask-ing myself that question. What am I to do? I mean should I go home tomorrow, or should I stay the extra week with-out pay? It is a pretty serious question to answer because 23 dollars is a lot of money to throw away, is it not?

But if I stay, I don't want to stay at Thoraeu's Walden! I know that sounds fantasdic after the way I raved the other night. I mean I want to stay at a different place, but still in the mountains. You will ask why I want to change, and I will answer because after your marvelous talk when you told me about your place up at Vele Pond, well, I got a little bit fed up with Thoraeu's Walden.

Somehow after what you said it seemed like I wasn't living up to my plan to be like Riva, the girl in Green Mansions. *I felt like there was something different in the country where she was living in than the one where Thoraeu's Walden* is. *That is to be expected of course because the Adirandacks are one place and Venezwela another.*

Now, Tommy, I wonder if I could make you a proposition. My boss in Newark where I work, he always says a bonna fida proposition. I still have 30 dollars left out of my vacation money. Why not take me as a boarder up at your pond?

This is the way I look at it. You said you had a lot of room up there, and I would stay 1 week and pay you whatever you would ask for. Up to 30 dollars. But it would not be that much, would it?

I could help you do the cooking, and would it not be fun climbing up and down the hills together and swimming? You can be sure I am not a bother, but if you don't want me around the house I could easily camp out in the woods. I could get some things in Warrensburg, a frying pan and a coffee pot, and blankets you could loan me, I suppose.

How awfully thrilling it sounds! Camping out in the woods with a campfire going, and little me laying there with only my thoughts for company! I never mind being left alone. I like it quiet so as I can think, and when am I ever alone in a city like Perth Amboy or even Newark?

What do you say, Tommy? I hope you will not disappoint me because I have my heart set on it. So please write

me a letter at once, otherwise I have to leave soon, and tell
me what you think. I am so excited I can hardly wait to
read what you have to say.

Ever Sincerely,
Rose (Riva) Bernard

—Leaving the Post Office, I drove down the pike toward the Viele Pond fork. As I passed Nate's house, I saw him on his knees in front of a long trough that stood in the shade of an elm. I backed the car into the driveway.

—'Where's the uniform, Nate?'

—'Last I seen of it, it was hanging on a peg in the cowbarn. That cap was starting in to sting me like it was stuffed with hornets, so I quit the job all of a sudden. Didn't nobody tell you?'

—'Sure you aren't making a big mistake? Swell clothes like that don't come with every job, you know.'

—'I'm not making no mistakes. I'm going fishing.'

—'Where's your ambition?'

—'Don't have any.'

—'Don't you want to succeed?'

—'Sure, but first I'm going fishing.'

—'Where?'

—'Up the bridge near Thurman. The bass is back there strong as ever.'

—'And you weren't going to tell me?'

—Nate smiled. 'I didn't guess you had so much fun last time. You looked kind of—what do you call it?—ambitious.'

—I smiled too. 'Last time was last time.'

—'Let's go, then, man! I got a minnie here for you that'll catch the biggest bass God ever made. He's King of the Minnies. Soon's I wipe this grease off of my hands, I'll bail him out and show you.'

—'Here, Nate,' I said, reaching into my pocket and taking out a crumpled ball of paper. 'Wipe your hand on this....'"

✤ ✤ ✤

Platt:… Saturday night after Saturday night I used to hang around Polk's store, watching the regulars play checkers, but the one living soul that talked to me was Polk himself, and he only wanted to say he was closing up for the night. All week long I'd swear I was never going to stick my nose in there again as long as I lived, but when the next Saturday rolled around, there I'd be, setting on the same keg of nails from late afternoon to closing time.

That'd been going on for about a year, and I was there as usually one night when a young fellow come in that I never seen before. All the regulars knew him, though, and give him the time of day like he was a regular too. I watched him when he went over to the counter to tell Polk what he wanted, and after the storekeeper turned away to pull down some cans, this young fellow spotted me on my nailkeg. He looked at me for a couple of seconds, and finally he spoke up.

"Isn't your name Platt?" he said. "Aaron Platt?"

"Yes," I said, and I seen that everyone in the place was watching us.

"I don't suppose you remember me."

I shook my head. "No, I don't."

"I'm Tom Paulhan."

I tried to place the name, but I couldn't.

"You still don't remember?" he said.

"No."

"I'm surprised, Aaron. If I'd knocked a man's tooth out, I think I'd know him when I saw him again."

"I knocked your tooth out?"

He smiled. "Yes, a long time ago. We went to school together, and one day I laughed at you for something or other—I don't recall what it was any more—and you belted me across the mouth."

"If you know me from school, then it must be a long time ago. It's all of fifteen years since I quit."

Polk come over with Paulhan's provisions. "Anything else, Tom?"

"No," Paulhan said. "Just put the stuff in a bag and take it out to the car, will you?"

"Sure, Tom. Charge it?"

"Yes," Paulhan said, and he turned back to me. "Why'd you quit?"

I didn't know what to say to that, but I was so tickled to be talking to somebody that I didn't want Paulhan to go away, and yet I simply couldn't think of a thing to keep him there. I just sat where I was, staring up at him.

He stuck his chin out at the people on the other side of the store. "Know anybody here?"

"All, I guess, but none to talk to."

"Come on over, then, and I'll introduce you." I didn't want to go, but he took me by the arm. "These rubes won't bite you. They'll *back*bite, though, and that's all you have to watch out for."

We went around the tables and waited for a game to end. Then Paulhan said, "This is Aaron Platt. You know his father, don't you?"

One of the men looked up from the board, where he was setting out the checkers for a fresh game. "You bet, Tom," he said.

Paulhan said, "What do you mean—you bet?"

The man was looking down again. "I just mean—you bet we know Amram Platt."

Paulhan turned to me. "That's Emerson Polhemus, Aaron."

I put my hand out across the checkerboard, but all Polhemus done was push it aside a little because it was over some of the squares that he had to put the pieces on.

"And his opponent here," Paulhan said, "is Sam Pirie. We went to school with his daughter Esther."

I still had my hand out like some cheap present that nobody wanted; Pirie didn't take it either. One after another Paulhan introduced me to all the men in the crowd—Smead the sheriff, Bertrand the druggist, Mansfield the fellow that had the dry-goods store, Hustis—every one of them, and for all they seen of my hand stuck out there right under their noses, it might just as well of been in my pocket.

"What's the matter with you people?" Paulhan said.

Mansfield looked up. "Why nothing, Tom. What makes you think there is?"

Paulhan said, "You give me a good stiff pain in the prat—the whole lot of you!"

Pirie doublejumped Polhemus. "I don't give nobody a stiff pain in the prat."

Smead said, "Me neither."

"Come on, Aaron," Paulhan said, and we started for the door.

Somebody said, "Now, what's that Platt boy feisting around here for all the time?"

I swung about. "Who said that?"

Polhemus spoke up, "I did, boy. What makes you ask?"

"I just wanted to say I hope you drop dead, that's all."

For a couple of seconds nobody budged or made a sound. Then Paulhan laughed out loud. "He won't, though," he said. "He'll live to bury the two of us. Let's get out of here."

We'd no sooner got outside than what I turned and started back. Paulhan grabbed me.

"Where are you going?" he said.

"Back in there and hammer that Polhemus through the floor."

"Don't be a fool, Aaron."

"That old stinkweed thinks he's too good to talk to me!"

"Start anything with old man Polhemus, and the first thing you know Smead'll clap you in jail. Forget it."

"Forget hell! That God damn bunch of dirtfarmers—who the hell do they think they are?"

"Jesus Christ Himself—every last one of them."

"Where do they come off acting like I don't have any right to show my face in the village? Take your hands off, Paulhan! I'm going to settle this once and for all!"

Paulhan dragged me back. "The only thing you're out to settle is your own hash...."

"What's the matter, Tom?"

A young woman was setting in the front seat of an old open-top Ford that stood in the roadway. There was a lawn between us and then the width of a flagstone walk, but her face was very clear in the light that come through the windows of the store. Nobody would of picked her face out to paint for a calendar, and yet it was the kind of a face that made you keep on looking at it, and the more you looked, the more you wondered why you didn't think it was pretty in the first place.

"What's the matter, Tom?" she said again.

"Oh, nothing. Just a little dispute, that's all. Come over here, Aaron— Grace, I want you to meet Aaron Platt; Aaron, this is Grace Tennent...."

Polhemus: Wait a minute. What did you say the woman's name was?

Platt: Tennent—Grace Tennent. Why?

Polhemus: I didn't hear you.

Jessup: Go on, Platt.

Platt: She put out her hand and said, "I'm glad to know you."

Paulhan said, "Miss Tennent's a cousin of mine. She comes from Inlet."

"Where's that?"

"Over on Fourth Lake."

"I never been further than Lake George. What kind of country you got over there at Inlet, Miss?"

"Pretty much the same as this."

"You going to stay here long?"

The girl looked at Paulhan.

"That depends," he said. "Grace came here to take care of my mother—she got sick while I was up at Harry's place on Viele Pond a few weeks ago. I had to come down right away, but it takes a woman to look after a woman, so I sent for Grace. In a way, it's lucky this sickness came on before the fall; I'd have been God knows where by this time. As it is, I'll have to stay around until my mother gets better."

The girl said, "Maybe she won't get better, Tom."

He said, "Sure she will. She's only sixty."

The girl didn't say anything to that, but she kept on watching Paulhan.

"Well, I guess I'll be moving," I said. "Good night, Paulhan. Glad to of met you, miss."

"I am too," she said.

"Good night, Aaron," Paulhan said.

I walked up the road towards the Tavern. Back of me I heard the Ford move off, and I listened to the sound of the motor till there was nothing left to listen to, but I didn't turn around.

It was still pretty early for a Saturday night, only about nine o'clock, so I went in the Tavern to get something to eat. I took a seat over in a corner and ordered up a piece of pie and a cup of coffee, but the food sat in front of me for quite a while before I touched it. I'd just started when the door opened, and a girl walked in. She stopped just inside of the place, and from the way the other people looked her over, I figured she was new to Warrensburg. Finally she come and set at the table next to mine, and then the others went back to drinking their Bevo and Nehi.

We got to talking when she said would I pass her the bill of fare. She was a waitress, I found out, and she just come up from Saratoga on the evening stage.

"They laid me off down at the Grand Union when the race meet wound up a couple of weeks ago," she said, "and I been looking high and low for another job ever since. Yesterday I heard the Inn across the road needed some extra help, so I took a chance and came on up to this Godforsaken dump."

"You get the job?"

"I got it, all right, only the clerk said I didn't have to show up till morning, and when I ast him about eating he said the kitchen was closed up for the night. Some dump, this is. I'm surprised they don't pull in the sidewalks when it gets dark." She opened her pocketbook and started hunting for something. "I don't even get put up at the Inn. I got to board out." She handed me a scrap of paper. "You know where this joint is?"

I looked at the paper. "Yes," I said. "It's on the Viele Pond road."

"Wherever *that* is! The clerk said this Bennett takes on boarders."

"His farm's quite a ways from here. You figuring on walking it?"

"I don't see any hansom cabs around. Sure I'm going to hoof it—and I got a suitcase to lug along with me, just in case it ain't far enough to get me winded."

"I can give you a hand if you want. I don't have anything particular to do."

"Say, that's mighty white of you!"

"It's no trouble."

"I'll make it up to you some time, farmer."

"I'm not looking for any pay."

She took a look at me, and then she said: "I didn't mean I was going to give you money."

"You want to go now, miss?"

"Sure."

After we settled up the bill at the Tavern, she took me around the back of the Inn to get the suitcase, and then we started out for Bennett's. From the Inn to the bridge we didn't come across a single person, and not a car passed going either way. It happened to be a warm night, the kind you sometimes get the early part of September, or else the girl would of rattled herself to pieces in the rig she was wearing—a lightweight summer dress and a coat about as thick as the lining I had in mine.

She stopped on the bridge and looked down at the water. "What river is this?" she said.

"The Schroon. It joins up with the Hudson a couple of miles further along."

"It goes pretty fast."

"The water's low right now. You ought to see this little river when it's bringing the snow with it. It washed the bridge away once."

"You don't tell me," she said, and then she turned around and leaned her back against the railing. "It's a nice night."

"It's pretty near always nice this time of year, only maybe tonight it's a bit warmer than usually."

"Got any cigarettes?"

"No, miss, but you can roll one if you know how." I handed her a sack of Bull.

She knew how. She took a sheet of Riz La from the little pack that was pasted onto the bag, and she shook out just the right amount of tobacco, and in a couple of seconds she was licking a cigarette as neat as any tailormade I ever seen. I struck a match on one of the struts and cupped it up to her face, and she put her hands around mine while I lit the cigarette. She took a deep drag and then let the smoke come out in a long thin blast.

"What's a matter?" she said when she seen me watching her. "Don't you smoke cigarettes?"

"Sometimes."

"Here, take mine. I'll roll another."

We stood there in the dark, smoking our cigarettes and listening to the sound of the water. Every now and then an owl sounded off in the woods, and once a dog bayed from up the village way, but otherwise it was very quiet, so quiet, I remember, that I could hear the girl breathing.

I thought about what'd happened at Polk's a little while before, and I thought about Tom Paulhan and how he'd been the first villager to be friendly to me in years and years, and little by little that day at school come back to mind—the map on the blackboard, the boys and girls, Mister Quinn using the pointer to trace out the boundaries of New York, the pinhole that stood for Warrensburg *there's only a lot of little dots with words alongside of them. Where's the people and the houses and the animals, and where's all the rivers and hills and woods and fields? I can see them things with my own eyes when I look out of that window, but only a dunce would say they was on the map.* And with fifteen years to put between that day at school and that night on the bridge, I could still hear those children hooting at me because they thought *I* was such a dunce.

I thought about Paulhan again and wondered whether I still felt the same way about him, and then I thought about that girl of his, Grace Tennent....

She lived in his house. She was there all the time, and no matter where he went, no matter what he done with himself all day—whether it was fishing at Vicle Pond, or hunting rabbits around the playedout farms on Harrington Hill, or just laying under a tree and looking at the sky—no matter when he showed up, she'd be waiting there at the house for him.

I wondered whether he went out at night—he'd of been foolish if he did. After the girl puts his mother to bed, I was thinking, she comes back to the parlor, and the two of them sit there for hours, talking to each other about everything under the sun. She's across the table from him, not looking at him but busy with something or other, and he watches her for as long as she cares to stay, seeing the lamplight on her hair, seeing the way it moves when she moves her head, seeing her mouth and her eyes and her fingers, and it's a treat just to hear her speak even if he only listens to the sound and not the words, and when she finally goes upstairs he can stay where he is for a while, making out she's not in *her* room but *their* room, making out he can follow her whenever he's ready. He'd of been foolish if he went out at night.

Having that girl in the same house was like being married to her, except for one thing, except for sleeping in different rooms, but up to bedtime everything was exactly the same. She cooked for him, she mended and washed his clothes, she cleaned the house and kept the place as neat as if it was her own. That was the only difference—having two bedrooms instead of one.

But suppose there wasn't even *that* difference! Suppose he'd stopped her once when she said good night and headed for the stairs. Suppose he ast her if she felt like taking a little walk down the road—and suppose she *did* feel like it. They didn't go very far, maybe; they sat down in the soft thick grass somewheres up the bank. He'd meant to say something, he'd meant to keep on talking just like they was still in the parlor, but out there in the dark with the girl so close to him, he couldn't think of anything to talk about; he could only look at her. And suppose looking at her wasn't enough any more. Suppose he put his arms around her, suppose he found that looking wasn't enough for her any more, either....

I felt a hand touching my shoulder. I didn't move, and for a little while the girl's hand stayed where it was, like it come there by accident; but then it went on up to my throat and slid along till it reached my face; and there she pressed harder with her fingers, curling them to get the feel of my skin under her nails; and then they was digging at my lips; and then all of a sudden she swung about, come up close to me, and put her arms around my neck.

"Give us a kiss," she said.

I held back, but she pulled at me, at the same time rubbing her body against me, and then I couldn't help myself. I grabbed her, wishing she was somebody else, wishing I'd wake up in a little while and find out she wasn't just some stranger, but Grace,

Grace Tennent, wishing she was Grace Tennent—and I put my mouth down, and it was Grace's mouth I was kissing hard enough to mash her lips out flat on her teeth, and it was Grace's body my hands was fumbling around with and feeling out in the dark like a blind man's. I remember I was surprised to find so little to the girl's body.

She pulled away from me, wiping her mouth with the back of her hand. "How far is it to Bennett's?" she said.

"About a mile and a half," I said, and my voice was far away, like it come from a mouth on the other side of the bridge.

"Let's get on up there." The girl turned away and started off alone.

I waited for a couple of seconds, listening to her high heels hammer at the planking, and then I picked up the suitcase and followed her. She was waiting for me at the Thurman fork.

"Which way?" she said, and I nodded to the left.

When we got to the top of the first rise, I stopped to give her a chance to catch her breath, and when we set out up the next grade, the long steep one that takes you up to the Harrington Hill shoulder, I told the girl to hang onto my arm. We went along that way for a while, and finally she put her arm around my waist. I took ahold of her with my free hand, but every so often I'd have to switch sides with her so's I could shift the suitcase.

We'd been climbing like that for about five hundred yards when we was stopped dead in our tracks by a fogbank as thick as clay. It was so solid you could put your hand out and feel it weigh down on you, and when you opened your mouth you felt like you'd bit off a chunk of snow. It clogged your nose and throat like fur, and even when you took a good deep breath you wasn't satisfied; something was pressing on your chest, and you couldn't seem to swell it out all the way. Your eyes was good for about a yard; beyond that, the whole world went away.

Alongside of me a dim face dangled in the air like a paper lantern. I dropped the suitcase and reached out for the girl, and when I felt her body I pulled it towards me. She put her hands on the sides of my head and dragged it down, fixing her mouth on mine like she meant to eat me, like she was going to tear me apart with her teeth. Her face was cold and damp, and her coat was covered with little fine drops of fog that smeared out to sheets of cold water when I run my hands over them. Her hair was wet too, and it felt like it was melting when I put my face in it. I didn't know what to do with my hands; I kept flapping them all over the girl's body like I was trying to beat out a fire.

"What're you waiting for?" she said. "What're you waiting for, you big rube?"

I couldn't make myself hold still. My legs felt like they was going to shake out from under me; there wasn't any caps onto my knees, and I was afraid that any minute they'd fold over the wrong way. I had ahold of the girl's arms, and I could feel her thin little muscles standing out like frozen cord, and then they went soft in my fingers, and she lifted her head up and spoke right in my mouth.

"For God's sake, what're you waiting for?"

I picked her up as easy as if she was a pillow and started for the roadbank with her, but I couldn't see my way in the fog, and I was just walking and walking till I tripped on a rock at the edge of a ditch, and we fell down in the road. I landed on my elbows, or else I'd of killed the girl, coming down on her with all my weight. I tried to get up, but she wouldn't let me. She grabbed me by the hair, and she pulled me down till I was laying on top of her right there in the road, in the wet sand, in the fog....

I crept away a little and flopped down on my face, with my hands stretched out flat on either side. I was all wrung out like a twist of wet wash, and so tired that it was all I could do to breathe. The damp road had a good smell coming up out of it, like earth that you turn up on the shady side of a building. I dug my fingers in it, and it was fat and crumbly, and it went to my head like a field after a summer shower. I sucked in the smell as deep as I could, and laying there on my belly, I felt like I was trying to shove the world away from me with my chest, and after a while I found out I could do it, I found out I could breathe as deep as I wanted, and then I wasn't tired any more.

"Hand me that sack of tobacco," the girl said, "and I'll make us a couple of more cigarettes."

We sat there in the road, blowing smoke at the fog till the heels of the butts begin to burn our mouths, and all that time neither of us said a word. The fog was getting thinner in the meanwhile, and I was catching flashes of blue through holes in the gray. It was still pretty thick down near the road, though, but when I heard the trees shaking, I knew the wind would soon take it away downhill.

The girl said, "Let's go."

She waited for me to get the suitcase, and then she followed me up the road. I didn't stop till we reached Bennett's. I put the suitcase down at the gate and stood around for a couple of seconds, not knowing what to do or say.

The girl said, "Good night, and thanks for the favors."

I said goodnight too, and I moved off down the road, but she come running after me and got me by the hair again and tore my face down for some more kissing. When I begin to get excited, she pushed me off.

"Not now," she said. "Some other time."

"When?" I said. "When?"

"Any time you want, only not now."

"I don't come over the village till next Saturday night."

"Make it Saturday, then. Meet you at the same place."

I waited till I couldn't hear her shoes on the gravel any more, and then I headed down the slope....

⚜ ⚜ ⚜

—...Leaving Polk's, I drove down the road toward Lake George. As we neared the Schroon River bridge, Grace pointed off to the right.

—'Isn't that the way to Viele Pond?' she said.

—'Yes,' I said. 'Why?'

—'I'd like to go up there.'

—'Now—at night? It'll be pretty cold.'

—'I don't care about that.'

—I slowed down to take the shaky trestle in low gear. The headlights splintered on the whitewashed supports.

—'1874,' Grace said, reading the date on the end beam overhead.

—From the bridge to the Harrington Hill shoulder, I had to keep my eyes on the road every inch of the way. With Bennett's behind us, we headed up another grade, and at the crest the lamps picked out the iron railings of the hill graveyard.

—'That's where all the Bennetts are buried—most of them, anyway,' I said. 'Under the oak in the middle lies the first Bennett that came to America. His headstone reads: 1749-1848. In the same row are the graves of his five sons and three daughters, every one of whom died before the old man. I remember climbing that fence once and looking for the mother's stone, but I couldn't find it.'

—I stopped the car beyond the cemetery. 'The whole mountain falls away from here,' I said. 'In the daytime the little curved strips of road below you are only boomerangs lying in the grass, and Warrensburg itself is so small that it looks like a scatter of cracked stones. The Schroon is as fine as a wire, and when the sun hits it, a long section of the wire glows like a great spark. Up north, the mountains turn blue in the late afternoon, range after range of them so far away that they look like flagstones of slate stacked against an orange wall.'

—I started the car again. The road cut away from the shoulder and entered a narrow valley. 'All this in here was burnt out years ago,' I said. 'There's nothing left but an orchard of poles. On both sides of us the hills are gray. The ground, the trees, the rocks—all of them are the rusted gray of longdead ashes.'

—Beyond the charred grove, the country drooped downhill. I coasted the car, slicing the cool damp curtains of air hanging across the gap that the road made in the forest. Through the trees on the left now, there were tinfoil flashes of the Pond, and then, as we rounded a turn, we saw the dull tin roof of the lodge. I ran the car into a clearing and switched off the motor and lights. There was no wind. The only sound was an occasional ticking of the cooling engine.

—Grace spoke in a whisper, as if she were respectful of the silence. 'It's beautiful here,' she said.

—'Yes, it is.'

—'Who owns it?'

—'A fellow in Warrensburg—Harry Reoux.'

—'And he let you stay here all last summer?'

—'Yes.'

—'He must be a pretty good friend of yours.'

—'Oh, I don't know. A lot of poachers come over from Luzerne, and I suppose he wanted somebody around to warn them off.'

—'Did you see any?'

—'No, but some were probably around. This tract's a couple of rifleshots across the widest part.'

—'What did you do with your time, then?'

—'Nothing much.'

—'What did you do?'

—'Why do you ask?'

—'I want to know. What did you do?'

—'I went fishing quite a lot.'

—'And when you weren't fishing?'

—'I just sat around.'

—She looked off into the trees. 'It's a nice place to sit,' she said.

—'The nicest I know of—and best of all, Harry's kept it just as it was when his father gave it to him.'

—'What does he use it for?'

—'Hunting, mostly. He comes up here for a couple of weeks every fall.'

—'And that's all?'

—'Yes. What else would he do with a place like this?'

—'Give it away. Sell it.'

—'He'd never do that—he likes it too much. At one time or another practically everybody in Warrensburg was after him to sell off a section, but as far as I know he's still got every acre of the original tract. One fellow got old trying to buy the two hundred acres that adjoined his farm. That was Walter Pell, who used to have the place a couple of miles further in. Even after they sent his son Trubee to Dannemora for killing a man, he kept after Harry for some of the land, figuring, I suppose, that Trubee'd come back to farming when he finished out his term. Well, the old man died last year, and Trubee's still in prison, but these ten thousand acres haven't changed hands yet, and they never will.'

—'What would you do if you owned the place?'

—'What would I do?'

—'Yes.'

—'That's hard to say.'

—'Why?'

—'I don't want to own it.'

—'I thought you liked it so much.'

—'I do, but that has nothing to do with owning it.'

—'It might have—if Reoux told you to keep off.'

—'He'd never do that.'

—'But suppose he did.'

—'I'd find some place else.'

—'Without wanting to own that other place, either?'

—'I don't have to own a thing to enjoy it. The Pond, the lodge, the ground this car's standing on, the car itself—they all belong to Harry Reoux. I have the use of them, though, and that's all anyone ought to ask for.'

—'How about Reoux?'

—'If he wants property, that's his affair. It's nothing to me how much land, cattle, lumber, jewelry, and money he has—as far as I'm concerned, all that stuff is junk. I've never really owned anything in my life. ... You want to see the Pond?'

—The path crossed a clearing and entered a grove of pines, and there it lost itself in an ankledeep rug of needles. We went through the grove to the old beaverdam, where Stewart Brook started down the long rock staircase into Pell's hollow. A broad hedge of cat tail rimmed the Pond; inside this was a great flat washer of lilypads; in the center, in the open water, a quarter-moon rode the ripples like a melonrind. From a marsh at the far side of the Pond, a loon sounded off.

—'The loons are late this year,' I said. 'They're generally gone by the beginning of September.'

—We sat for a long time at the edge of the pinegrove, listening to the Stewart water tumble over stones.

—Finally Grace spoke. 'I know now why you like this place so much. There are no people about, and it's quiet ....'

—'Why do I always go away?'

—'Don't you know?'

—'This is the first time I've ever wondered. There's something peculiar about country, about *all* country: any one part of it is the same as all parts. One tree is all trees, one rock all rocks, one flower every flower that ever grew. Out in that Pond there are thousands of waterlilies; they're closed now, but when the sun comes up, every single one of them will open; and when the sun goes down, every single one of them will close again. That'll go on until the lilies die or the sun stops rising. How much can you say for that process, how many times can you describe it, how long can you stand it without beginning to suspect that you've been watching an endless belt of identical clay targets? I've lived in cities, I've lived in many cities, and my windows overlooked many forests, but they were forests of telephone poles. In the wilderness of those backyards, there was always one tree; its bark had long ago been hacked away, and its branches were a trap for years of leaves, rubbish, clotheslines, and lynched boxkites. From where we are now, I can see a thousand trees, but am I expected to become that many times as excited?'

—She said, 'You say you always go away, and I can understand that, but why do you always come back?'

—'I don't know,' I said. 'I just do.'

—For a long time I sat still, staring out over the water. The image of the moon no longer floated in the clear; it was smeared across the wet dishes of the lilies. The Pond was so dark that it merged with the stadium of woods surrounding it. The night was vastly quiet, remote from the small level music of insects, the broken music of breaking water, the diminished baying of a distant dog.

—And I turned, knowing that she had been watching me, knowing that she had been waiting for me to turn back to her, and with my hands on her body, with nothing between them and her flesh but warm thin layer of muslin, with my fingers telling the little embroidered crosses that covered the entire bodice of the dress, remembering for me the yellow and green pattern *the yellow over green, the yellow over green* that many washings had here and there blurred to blue, with my fingers pressing deeper as they moved to the underarm hollows where, in the heels of my palms, I felt the detaining mounds of her breasts, with my mouth on her mouth, with my body on her body—I knew that I was throwing away the one thing that I valued, the one thing....

—A fog was tumbling slowly down the hills beyond the Pond and spreading toward us across the water.

—'We'd better go, I said.'

—'Yes.'

—'While we can still see our way down the...'

—'Yes,' she said. 'Yes, Tom....'

✤ ✤ ✤

Platt: ... Doc Slocum said, "Where'd you pick it up, son?"

"Pick up what?"

"I mean who've you been out with lately?"

I told him about the waitress from the Inn.

"She the only one?" he said.

"Yes."

"Then that's were you got it. Don't you know better than to take up with any tramp that happens to be passing through town?"

"She wasn't a tramp, Doc."

"No? Well, you got pretty good proof that she was."

"She looked like a decent sort to me."

"They all look decent to boys your age. What's her name?"

"You have to know that?"

"Yes."

"The first name's Agnes. I didn't ask the family name, but I will when I see her tonight."

He grabbed me by the lapels of my coat and yanked me up out of the chair till my face was right under his. "You don't see her tonight or any other night—you hear me? I'll attend to *that* for you. She'll be in Warrensburg from now till the next bus goes through either way. You, son, you're not seeing any more women till the snow flies. Your seeing *me*, though, every night in the week at just this time. You understand that?"

"Yes, Doc," I said.

"You sure? *Every night!*"

"Yes, Doc."

"All right, then. Now, do you do any drinking?"

"Some. A snort of cider once in a while."

"Cut it out."

"Why? Where's the harm in a little cider?"

"Cut out the drinking, I said, and cut out sharp food too."

"But I want to know why I can't...."

"Listen, son, all *I* want to know is whether you're going to do what I say. If not, you can try that new doctor they got down to Lake George. You going to go by what I tell you?"

"Sure, Doc."

"Take off your pants and lay down on that sofa—and don't holler when I get to work on you."

"I don't holler."

"How's your father?"

"Spry as a goat."

"Tell him I said for him to go have a stroke."

"Glad to."

It was dark by the time Slocum finished up with me, and I walked the best way I could down the pike towards home. Quite a few cars and buggies was on the road, and I wondered where everybody was making for till I got down by the church, and then I see there was some kind of a celebration going on. I don't know why, but I hung around for a while, and finally I seen Paulhan drive up in his Ford. The people stood on both sides of the footpath, and he handed Miss Tennent out of the car and walked her inside the church. Both of them was togged out in their best, and then I knew what the celebration was for.

I stayed outside. I sat on the steps in the dark, and through the open windows come the sound of Mister Titus' voice.

"... The occasion of our gathering here tonight is one of the most joyous in the Christian calendar—the joining together in holy wedlock of a man and a woman—and yet I cannot refrain from pointing out the necessity of tempering our rejoicing with solemn reflection on the inscrutable ways of the Lord. One short month ago, in a distant country, a comely stranger left her abode and began a journey in search of employment, and it was as an humble servant in the house that she came to our hamlet to live under the roof of Thomas Paulhan. Standing before me now, at the side of Thomas Paulhan, is this same wayfarer, but no more is she a stranger, and no longer is she a servant in the house. She stands here as the betrothed of her former master, his equal in all things, his companion in all things, his partner in all things, and when the two, which shall be one flesh, leave this house of God, there shall be nothing save death which shall put them asunder. Verily, I say unto you, the ways of the Lord are inscrutable ... ."

He sounded the same over a coffin. I got up and walked around to the graveyard, and there I couldn't hear him talking through that allyear catarrh any more. I stretched out on a bench, surrounded by stone angels—little ones for children, big ones for grownups, and all of them with names, dates, and pomes on them—and I thought about the cheesy hunk of granite setting over my mother's head ... .

The ceremony was finished. Everybody piled out of the church and lined up again along the walk, waiting for Paulhan to come through with his wife. When they did, they had to run the gauntlet; rice sprinkled down on them from all sides, and a couple of old shoes bounced off of Paulhan's back before he could get to the door of his car. There was a lot of hollering and laughing and then more rice and shoes, and finally Paulhan drove off, dragging a string of tin cans with him along the pike ... .

⚜   ⚜   ⚜

—'... I enjoyed it, Grace—I can't think of anything I ever enjoyed as much. And yet when I try to tell you what I did, when I try to turn the pleasure into words for you to turn again into pleasure, there's hardly anything for me to say. It's like stripping a flower down in order to study the parts: you have the parts, but the flower is gone. Day after day I did nothing but go for a walk in the woods. I followed the roads until I'd passed the last farmhouses, and then I headed through the trees in whatever direction I happened to fancy. In the fall I liked to make for the Pond because that was the one place, after the gunners were out, where I knew I could still flush a few partridge, and several times I did, coming on the birds sunning themselves in the red and yellow fire of fallen leaves, or powdering their feathers in the dust of the road. Once I saw a gallinule tipping in the shallow water of the marsh, and once an osprey riding the aircurrents like a kite. After the first snow fell, I kept to the lower ground and trailed sign. I hardly ever managed to track the animals down—they were a little too good for me—but it was exciting work, and not all the excitement lay in making a score. It was like exploring an unknown road—it was better than that. This kind of road was aimless, and there'd never be an end to it until you stopped hunting for the end—which would be when you fell flat on your face and went to sleep in the snow....'

—Without looking up from the basket of sewing that she had in her lap, Grace said, 'When are you going away, Tom?'

—'I like things that've been abandoned,' I said, 'I like discarded clothes, deserted houses, the red skeletons of broken machinery, an old logging road with the corduroy eaten away and softened to punk. I like to find things that have no value, that lead you nowhere, that can serve no useful purpose—and that's why I enjoyed that little game I played with the animals in the snow....'

—'When are you going away, Tom?'

—'Why don't you say what you're thinking?'

—'What's that, Tom?'

—'That I'm a nogood bum.'

—'I don't think you're a nogood bum.'

—'I haven't done a lick of work since the day we were married, and I probably never will. Some day I'm going to walk out of that door and leave you in the lurch, I'm going to go sightseeing and have a good time, and you're going to stay behind and get along the best way you can. If I'm not a bum yet, I'll be one sooner or later, and you know it. What I can't understand is why you keep on being good to me.'

—'You can't understand that?'

—'And yet I have the feeling that you'll never change. I may never come back, but you'll always be expecting me. And if I do come back, no matter how long I've stayed away, you'll pick up again where you left off. You'll act as if I'd never quit you, as if I were only coming home after a day's work. You won't ask me to explain. You won't nag. You'll just put your arms around me and stop up my mouth with yours. You'll kiss me as if you were trying to give yourself away through your mouth. And later, when I say, "I wish I could tell you that I'm going to change, but that wouldn't be the truth. I may hang around for a while, but I'll clear out again before long, and you'll be right back where you were," you'll say, "I told you once that I didn't care what you did, and I tell you now that I don't care what you *don't* do, either. You don't have to work if you don't want to—I'll do the work, I'll get the money, I'll keep the house going. Sleep if you like, smoke, read the papers, walk around in the country all day, do *anything*—only come home at night. I'll be here as long as you're alive. You haven't done anything so terrible; you just went away for a few months, that's all. The only thing I care about is that you've come back. I knew you would, and you did. You're here now, and that's the end of it as far as I'm concerned." And when I say, "Because I came back once, you think I'll always come back? You think I won't do the same thing all over again—and stay away for good the next time?" you'll tell me, "I won't even ask you about that. You don't have to make me any promises. They wouldn't be any good, anyway, because if you ever want to go away again, they won't stop you. I'll do all I can to make it good for you here, so that maybe you won't *want* to go away, but if you *do* go, I'll know it was my fault—and you'll find me here when you get back. You'll always find me here." That's what you'll say, Grace. That's what you'll say, isn't it?'

—'Yes, Tom,' she said. 'That's what I'll say.'

—I went into the parlor then, and I closed the door behind me. I stood at the window, looking out at the melting snow that filled the rainwater ditches. On the gravel below me a few dry leaves moved in the scoops of wind, chafing each other. The bare trees hummed a little, their stiff branches retching as they swayed. I smoked my last cigarette and wondered what to do for the rest of the afternoon. I couldn't think of anything but sleep. I lay down on the sofa.

—It was easy to fall asleep on a day like that. All you had to do was close your eyes, and sleep began to roll over you like warm breeze; you shivered a little because you were so comfortable and because you knew it was raw outside; you hugged yourself as if you were trying to hold the warmth of the warm breeze of sleep close to your body; you hugged yourself for a very little while—and you were sleeping....

—When I woke up, the light was almost gone. The window was a block of confederate gray hanging against the union blue velour of the walls. I stared out over the little table that stood under the window, and my eyes were beginning to wobble again when I noticed that on the table, lying in an ashtray, there were two fresh packs of cigarettes and a box of matches.

—I don't know how long I lay there looking at those three little forms, but the parlor was completely dark when Grace came into the room. She walked quietly, as if she were afraid of disturbing me, and she didn't know that I was awake until she leaned over me and looked at my eyes. I reached up and touched her face, and then she sat down alongside me with the matches and a pack of cigarettes. She gave me a butt and struck a light for me, and I tried to see her in the flare, but it was cupped away from her face, and the light shone only on a braid of hair that she wore around her head like a quoit. I watched the spark shift along the coil until she took the match away and shook out the flame. She sat there, leaning against me a little and resting one of her arms on my chest, and we said nothing, and whenever I dragged on the cigarette I looked for her eyes in the spreading glow, but her head was turned away, and I couldn't see them. My own smarted as if I'd gotten soapy water into them—because I knew that I was leaving her that night ....

⚜ ⚜ ⚜

Platt: ... My father called me up to his room.

"What do you want?" I said.

"I think I'm going to die."

"I *know* you're going to die."

"Who told you?"

"Doc Slocum."

"I don't like that man."

"He ain't so wild about you."

"Why didn't you get that one from down to Lake George?"

"Otis? He wouldn't come."

"What's a matter? Ain't Platt money as good as the next man's?"

"Not to Otis, it wasn't. And Slocum didn't want to come, neither. Said it was high time you popped off."

"That's no way to talk. I sure hate to pay out good money to a man I don't like."

"He don't want any money."

"Since when did he get so independent?"

"Said he wouldn't think of taking money for watching you in your last sickness."

"No? Why not?"

"Said it was a pleasure."

"That's no way to talk."

"What did you bring me up here for? I got work to do."

"There's something I want to tell you."

"What?"

"I don't want to get buried up the hill there."

"Why not?"

"I been thinking it over, and the way I figure is a man's entitled to a good long rest after he's dead."

"You'll be getting that—don't worry."

"Not if somebody was to come along and plow up that field some time. I don't want any machinery snorting around over my bones."

"Where you want to get buried, then?"

"Down back of the church."

I looked at him for a minute. "That's religious ground."

"I won't be minding that after I'm cold."

"*You* won't, but how about the people in town that's got relatives laying there?"

"I don't see where they come in to put up any hollers. It ain't scriptural to bear a grudge against a dead man."

"So you don't want to lay up the hill?"

"No."

"Alongside of your wife?"

"No."

"The wife that worked so hard for you?"

"No."

"And your five dead children—you don't want to lay with them, neither?"

"No, I tell you. I want to lay in the churchyard."

"Why, you old bastard! Did you think I was going to stink up this farm by letting you rot in it?"

"That's no way to talk."

"Did you think I'd let you lay inside of a mile from my mother? You'll be God damn lucky if I don't cart your hide down to Albany and sell it to the hospital!"

"Now what would a hospital want with me after I'm dead?"

"They'd cut you up and find out what made you live so long."

"You wouldn't do that to your own father."

"Why wouldn't I?"

"It ain't religious."

"You think I'm religious?"

"It ain't a nice thing to get all cut up like a beef. It ain't decent. Promise me I'll get buried decent."

"I promise, but only because it'd be too much trouble to get you down to Albany. And about burying you on the hill, you can rest easy. You'll lay in the churchyard if I have to dig you in there in the dead of night. I got to go feed the stock now."

He died the next morning. I knew he was dead because he didn't holler down for his breakfast. I went up to have a look at him, and he was stonecold, and what galled me was the peaceful face he had onto him, just like he'd led one almighty Godfearing life. He was dead just the way you hear people talking about. In all his days he never once looked so softhearted as he done that morning. If you didn't know him, you'd be ready to swear by your life that he was the kindest man that ever drew breath.

When I went down to see the Reverend Mister Titus about getting a plot in the churchyard, he acted like I ast him to let me open up a cigarstand under the pulpit. He called in a bunch of the elders, and they'd probably of figured out a way to turn me down, only it happened there was people like Bennett and Reoux on the Board, and the others couldn't afford to show their real colors. In the long run they give in and sold me the ground, way off in a corner somewheres near the toolhouse.

I paid some Indian two dollars to dig me a nice deep hole, and then I went home and spent the rest of the day building a coffin out of the lumber from an old privy. I buried my father the next afternoon. It was a fine sunshiny day, and all the snow was gone, even from the shady hollows in the woods. The grass was coming up in little soft patches like mold, and on some of the trees the buds was busting open and showing green.

The Indian was waiting for me at the open grave, and the two of us unloaded the coffin and shoved it in the hole. It got away from us and turned over sideways, and then all of a sudden the Indian turned tail and took to his heels, running like all hell to get out of the graveyard. Me, I was a long way from smelling brimstone. As long as the coffin was out of sight, I didn't give a hoot how the devil it laid in the ground.

It was a pleasure to listen to them clods and stones bounce off of the side of the box. It was real music. Every time a spadeful rattled over the boards, the old man's hold onto me was getting weaker, and he was going further away, and pretty soon he'd be out of sight, and then I'd be shut of him for good and all. The dirt wasn't rattling any more—it was thumping....

"Who's getting buried?" somebody said.

I looked up, and standing alongside of me was one of the women from the village. She wore a cotton dress and lowheel shoes and a straw sunshade, and she had an empty basket slung over her arm. I'd seen her around a few times, but I didn't know her name. She was plainlooking, and I figured her to be about thirty or so.

I said, "My father."

"Oh, that's too bad. I'm sorry."

"Nothing to be sorry about, ma'am. It's Amram Platt."

"Amram Platt? I don't think I knew him."

"I thought everybody in town knew Amram Platt."

"Well, I only been in Warrensburg a couple of months. I was born and raised over to Stony Creek, but when my people died I had to come over here and live with my uncle."

"No use raking up the dead, then. My name's Aaron Platt, ma'am."

"Glad to know you," she said. "Mine's Dora Polhemus...."

Polhemus: Mention that name again, and old as I am, I'll come up and cane you, you lowlife!

Jessup: Sit down, man! If you've got anything to say, you can say it when Platt's through.

Polhemus: I'm not setting down to listen to this dog drag my niece's name in the mud!

Jessup: I agreed to hear Platt out, and that's what I'm going to do, no matter who gets hurt by it. Sit down!

Platt: I married the woman a couple of months later, and to this very day I'm still trying to figure out why. The wedding come off at the Polhemus house one night late in the summer, the ceremony being performed by Titus as usually, and afterwards there was a stingy feed for the people that'd been invited—there wasn't enough to go round even with half the people not showing up—but what with the cider somebody brung along, it wasn't so bad out there in back of the barn, and I was feeling kind of fairish when Polhemus took me aside and handed over the dowry. I'd never asked him for anything, but he'd been blowing for weeks about how the man that took his niece was going to get a thousand dollars in cash, so I was a little surprised when I come to count the money and only found a hundred and seventeen dollars in the purse. I never did learn how Polhemus reached an odd figure like that, but as God's my witness, that's what he give me....

Polhemus: You're not telling that story straight, you liar!

Platt: Supposing you point out what's a matter with it.

Polhemus: You just want to put me in a bad light—that's what's a matter!

Platt: How much was in that purse you give me the night I married Dora Polhemus?

Polhemus: A lot of money.

Platt: How much in dollars and cents?

Polhemus: More than you ever deserved.

Platt: I'm under oath here, Polhemus, and I just stated there was a hundred and seventeen dollars in the purse. You willing to say I was lying about that?

Polhemus: No, that's all there was, but the way you tell it...

Jessup: Hold on, there, Polhemus! You've admitted that Platt told the truth, and that's all the further I want this argument to go!

Polhemus: He didn't tell the whole truth.

Jessup: What did he leave out?

Polhemus: I forgot about the money being a little short when I give him the purse, but why don't he tell what I said when I met him in the village a couple of weeks later?

Platt: You want me to tell that? You said any time I felt like having the rest of the money, all I had to do was call on you for it—the whole eightythree dollars.

Jessup: Don't butt in again, Polhemus, or you'll be hearing the rest of Platt's story from your neighbors.

Platt: Getting back to that wedding night, the party busted up around ten o'clock. I lugged my wife's trunk downstairs and put it on the wagon, and then the two of us climbed up and waved goodbye to the crowd. There was some ricethrowing, but not an awful lot of it, the whole business being kind of halfhearted, anyhow—and we was on our way.

I wasn't in any tearing hurry, so I let the horse take his own good time about getting us home. It was a fine night, with the sky so loaded with stars that they seemed to weigh it down like an awning full of rain. I didn't think of anything particular till the horse's hoofs hit the planking of the Schroon River bridge, and then all at once I remembered another night, the one when I walked that waitress up Harrington Hill to Bennett's.

And for some reason or other I remembered a few more things: the little wagon that I'd built for myself, and my father kicking it to pieces because I'd nicked the blade of his knife; my first day at school, with everybody laughing at me because I couldn't understand the workings of a map; the extra chores that my father used to pile onto me to make me stop trying to learn something different than being a farmer, and how I finally come home that day and dumped my books in the privy; and then years and years of sweat, with my father's face in front of me day and night, day and night, day and night, till I prayed that he'd die before I grabbed up an axe and murdered him for spoiling my life.

I stopped the wagon in the middle of the bridge, making out that I just wanted to light my pipe, but what I really wanted to do was think some more about that other night. I remembered setting around the Tavern, and I remembered the woman coming in and taking the table next to me, and afterwards we stopped on the bridge to look down at the water, and she rolled us cigarettes, and when we'd smoked them we headed up the left fork into the fogbank, and we stood there blind, holding onto each other like we was the only two people left in the world, and she said: *What're you waiting for? What're you waiting for, you big rube?* ...

And there was one other thing about that night that I'd always remember. In front of Polk's store, setting in Paulhan's borrowed car, was Grace Tennent. I remembered her face, her hair, her clothes, the sound of her voice—and I remembered that she was Paulhan's wife.

There I was, setting alongside of my own. It was my wedding night, but it didn't mean a thing to me. I slapped the horse with the reins, and we moved off the bridge. We took the right fork.

We got out to the farm about eleven o'clock. It was a job dragging my wife's trunk upstairs, and when I finally got it to the landing, she told me to leave it there because she didn't know the house yet, and maybe she'd want to change the rooms around. I didn't care what she done with the rooms or anything else, so I went in the bedroom and started getting undressed.

She stood over by the window all the while, not looking at me and not making a move to take her own clothes off. I had my shirt and hard collar unfastened, and I was unbuttoning my shoes when all of a sudden I heard a loud thump, and there was my wife laying all stretched out on the floor. She didn't come to right away, so I got some water out of the pitcher and tried to make her drink it, but I couldn't pry her teeth open, let alone make her swallow. I figured she'd be all right if I left her alone for a little while, so I finished getting undressed, and after I put on my nightshirt I sat down and waited for the woman to show some signs of life.

I got tired of waiting, though, because it begin to look like she'd went right out of the faint and into a sound sleep without stirring a muscle. I thought the best thing to do was undress her and get her under the covers, so I picked her up off the floor and laid her down on the bed. I didn't like my job any too much, but there wasn't any help for it, and I got to work. The dress was fixed on with hooks, buttons and pins....

Polhemus: Are you going to let this man go on with that filth?

Jessup: I haven't heard anything filthy yet.

Polhemus: He's fixing to tell about everything that happened on his wedding night. I call that filthy!

Jessup: Then you've just got a filthy mind, that's all.

Titus: It's hardly my business to interfere in a legal proceeding, but if Mister Platt is about to reveal the secrets of the nuptial couch, then I'm afraid I'll have to make the same objection as Mister Polhemus. What transpires between a husband and wife is strictly...

Jessup: None of your business, just as you said at the start, Mister Titus—but it's *my* business, and I'll thank you to keep your nose out of it.

Titus: Your tone is offensive, Mister Jessup. Kindly bear in mind that although I wear the garb of a cleric, I happen to be a citizen of Warrensburg, and therefore I have as much to say in these proceedings as anyone else in this Hall.

Jessup: Which is exactly nothing, Mister Titus. The minute you step out of that little church of yours, you get about as much attention paid to you as the Pope of Rome. This is the law that you're butting into now, and if you don't sit down pretty God damn fast, I'll have a deputy throw you out on your back.... We're listening to you, Mister Platt.

Platt: After fiddling around with that dress for a couple of minutes, I managed to get enough of it open so's I could peel it down over the woman's legs, but there was still mighty far to go. First come some kind of a garment that looked like another dress, only it didn't have any sleeves or fancies onto it; it turned out to be a combination corsetcover and petticoat, and off it went like the dress. Next was the corset, a regular ironclad that would of turned back a charge of buckshot. It was hooked in front and laced in back, but before I could get to work on it there was a little matter of two more petticoats that had to be tended to. I got them loose after a while, but only with some uncommon backbreak, and then I tried my hand at taking off that layer of whalebone and steel. I wrassled with the machine for a good five minutes before I give it up as a bad job and slit the laces with my knife. That eased up the whole business, and I yanked it out from under the woman and chucked it onto the floor, and it rattled like sheetiron. There was still the shoes and stockings, but that was nothing compared to the rest. It was only when I come to take off the underwear that I balked; I couldn't make myself touch it. Figuring it was as good as a nightgown, I leaned across the woman to draw up the covers, and at just that minute she come back to life.

Finding me there bending over her, she was pretty near to fainting dead away again. She opened her mouth to let out a yell, but she was froze so stiff with fright that not a sound come out, and it looked like she was only yawning. I took hold of her hands and tried to calm her down, but she tore them away and folded them across her chest, grabbing herself tight like she had something there to hide.

"What's got into you?" I said.

She didn't answer. She just scrambled under the covers, and there she laid, buried to the chin and shivering fit to shake me off of the bed. I got sore at actions like that, so I took her by the shoulders and shook her even harder than she was shaking herself.

"What's a matter with you?" I said. "What're you carrying on about?"

"Where's my clothes?" she said. "Who took them off of me?"

"I did."

"What else did you do?"

"Nothing."

"What else did you do after you took off my clothes?"

"Nothing, I told you. What else *would* I do?"

"You did something else to me! You know you did!"

"You're working yourself up for nothing."

"You're lying! You did something dirty!"

"Listen, woman! I never laid a finger onto you, and the way you look to me right now I don't think I ever will!"

When I said that, she started in bawling like a baby. Her face got all screwed up like a dried apple, and with the tears coming down and washing out streaks in the rice powder, and with her hair all mussed up and laying over her eyes, she didn't look like thirty years old any more. She looked like what she was—a good fortyfive.

"For Christ's sake, shut up your hollering!" I said. Nobody's going to cut your throat. I don't want any part of you *that* bad!" And I grabbed up a blanket and one of the pillows, and I went in the other bedroom.

In the morning I went right on downstairs and fixed breakfast for myself, and I didn't see my wife till I come back to the house late in the afternoon. I took one look at her there in bed, still asleep and all coiled up like a cat, and then I turned my back on her and went over to the window. It was a gray day outside, and it weighed me down to think of the long string of gloomy gray days stretching out ahead of me, and for the first time I wondered how it was that I come to be chained to that old maid I'd brought home to be my wife. If I didn't bury my father in the churchyard, I'd never of met her. My father was an animal, and he didn't have any right to lay in the same ground with his family. I hated him, and that's why I got all tangled up with Dora Polhemus—I'd met her because I hated my father!

And I'd been fool enough to think that when I got him all covered up, I'd be done with him for the rest of my life! Why, he was stronger dead than most people are when they're alive! He was still riding over my mother like a harrow; he was still plowing her for a litter a year and still burying the crop up the hill like drowned kittens; he was still batting me across the mouth whenever I got in reach of his hand; he was still roaring his head off about me going to school; he was still being a weasel about thinking up ways to cheat me out of doing my homework.... He wasn't laying wormy in the ground—he was still parading around that farm, running it with that iron hand of his and that iron heart.

It was almost dark when I come away from the window, and I could just make out the skinny little grave that my wife's body made in the blankets. That minute was the turningpoint. I could of felt sorry for her, I could of gone over and sat down alongside of her and said nice things so's she wouldn't be ascared of me anymore, and maybe after a time we'd of worked out a way to get along with each other—or I could of been hard, like my father always was, and said the hell with it. I picked my father's way.

In all the five years that I was married to that woman, I never slept with her once. I had my rights by paying the Widder a dollar for it every Saturday afternoon ....

Titus: There's no Widow in *this* town!

Platt: No? One of your elders rents her the house she lives in.

Titus: Name him!

Platt: You really want me to do that?

Polhemus: Sit down, Mister Titus. Everybody here can see the man's lying.

Pirie: I'm not so sure about that, Emerson. Seems to me I heard something about there being a Widder in this here village.

Hustis: Me too, Sam. Who was it told us about it down to Polk's a ways back?

Pirie: I disremember, but I know it was *somebody.*

Polk: It was Broadbent, that drummer from Utica.

Pirie: Broadbent—that's who it was, all right!

Hustis: Now, what was it he said again, Sam?

Pirie: Well, he come in Polk's around nine o'clock that night, looking like he'd been trying to put out a forestfire all by himself.

I seen he was a bit peaked, so I said right out to him in front of the bunch of us, "Say, Broadbent, where you been that you look so fagged out?"

He said, "Up the road a piece, saying hello to a old friend of mine."

I said, "Well, you sure must of said it mighty hard. Only place you got any starch left into you is your collar."

He said, "It was the walk done me in."

I said, "What walk?"

He said, "From up the road to here."

I said, "How far's that?"

He said, "Couple or three miles."

I said, "Twothree mile? Let's see, now. Wouldn't that be pretty near all the way to Thurman bridge?"

He said, "It just about would, yes."

I said, "There ain't but one house that far out of town up Thurman way. Would that be the place where your friend's at?"

He said, "I guess it would, Sam."

I said, "I never been in that house, Broadbent. What's the name of the party lives in it?"

He said, "Now, to tell you the truth, I never did inquire. Ain't that funny—being friends with a person for so long, and not knowing the name?"

I said, "It's more than funny—it's damn peculiar. What's that person do for a living?"

He said, "It's funny about that too. I couldn't rightly say."

I said, "That's mighty uncommon—knowing a man that you don't know what he works at."

He said, "I didn't say the person was a man, did I, Sam?"

I said, "Come to think about it, you didn't. It's a woman, then, eh?"

He said, "I guess there ain't much else for her to be."

I said, "It's sure nice for you to be friendly with a woman owns her own house. That could lead to something."

He said, "Oh, I ain't thinking of getting married, Sam. And besides, it ain't her house."

I said, "What's that you're saying? The woman's living in somebody else's house!"

He said, "She pays rent."

I said, "She sure must be rich, then, if she can afford to pay rent."

He said, "No, she ain't rich."

I said, "It's a strange tale, Broadbent. Who's she rent the house from?"

He said, "The owner, I guess."

I said, "That's only natural, but what's his name?"

He said, "His name?"

I said, "Yes, his name."

He said, "It's ...."

Polhemus: We've had just about enough of this damn nonsense! Pirie's making up that story as he goes along!

Pirie: I'm surprised at you, Emerson. You know I wouldn't make up any stories ....

❧   ❧   ❧

—... I was sitting on a bench in the park, facing a lawn that sloped away to a cove in the lake. The wooden dark water lay flat in the windless afternoon, carrying a glittering powder of dust like the top of an enormous piece of furniture. Beyond the lake, hidden by trees, motorcars made rapid tides of sound on an asphalt roadway; and beyond the furthest trees rose the punctured face of the city. It was warm in the sun, and I felt sleepy, and all that kept me awake was the quick movements of a flicker as it hammered its scalped head at the lawn.

—There were footfalls in the grass. Someone sat down at the other end of the bench, and I heard the crumpling of paper, the grating of a match on stone, and a hissing flare, and then I smelled the always unusual fragrance of somebody else's tobacco. The drifting flavor was so pleasant that I turned a little and looked at the cigarette, at the bright blue smoke at the lighted end and the graybrown smoke at the other.

—'Have one?' the man said.

—I looked at him; he was holding out the pack to me. I took a cigarette and lighted it.

—'Thanks,' I said.

—'You from out of town?'

—'Yes.'

—'Whereabouts?'

—'Upstate. Warrensburg.'

—'This your first time in New York?'

—'I've been here before.'

—'You work here?'

—'No.'

—'Just on a trip, then.'

—'You can call it that.'

—'What do you do back home?'

—'Nothing.'

—'Nothing at all?'

—'Nothing.'

—A flock of mallards sailed around a rocky point in the lake, opening up giant arrowheads of intersecting ripples. The birds veered into the cove and coasted, some of them twisting suddenly to bore holes in their feathers, others tilting to feed underwater and looking like tiny sidewheelers going down by the bows.

—He said, 'It's a pleasure to do nothing once in a while.'

—'It's a pleasure all the time,' I said.

—He laughed. 'How long have you been at it?'

—'All my life.'

—'You're about thirty?'

—'A little less—and you?'

—'Just thirty, and retired—for the day.'

—'Why don't you retire for good?'

—'The usual reason.'

—'What's that?'

—'Duty.'

—'Never heard of it.'

—'Ever hear of being married?'

—'I'm married too.'

—'And it doesn't stand in your way?'

—'No.'

—'It does in mine.'

—'That's your fault.'

—'How?'

—'Don't let it.'

—'Just pick up and walk out?'

—'Don't even wait to pick up.'

—'Is that the way you did it?'

—I smiled. 'No, I think I picked up first.'

—'It's easy to talk about.'

—'And easy to do—if you're built that way.'

—I found a peanut on the walk. I shelled it and took it down to the bank of the lake, and the mallards converged like tugs around a liner. The nut was taken by a drake; he waited a few seconds for more and then shoved off, flashing his nightblue chevrons. I waved to the man on the bench and started to walk away. He came after me.

—'Where are you going?' he said.

—'No place.'

—'I'll go along for a while.'

—We crossed the Mall toward Columbus Circle, walking over a shadow that buried the deep soft grass. The setting sun hit the sides of the buildings south of the park, exploding on a hundred windowpanes and firing the ranks of glass like gunports in a broadside.

—'You'll stay here till you get tired of it, I suppose,' he said.

—'Never longer.'

—'That's the whole point, eh?'

—'Yes—otherwise I'd only be doing what you are.'

—We stood for a moment near the brokenarmed Maine Monument, watching the steel of traffic strike seven streams of sparks from the whirling flint of the Columbus column.

—'Let's go that way,' he said, pointing down the diagonal.

—And then for a long time there were only lights—the staring lights of trolleycars, the swinging lights of cornerlamps, the palpitating lights of photographers' windows, the crawling lights of traffic, the racing lights of electricsigns. It was the last of these, the electric antics, that dominated the display and filled the darkening sky. Lights gushed up into the evening, smeared, flowed, galloped, bobbed, shuttled, spun, jigged, and winked, and they blew up like rockets, radiated like ripples, foamed like surf, and fled like mercury, and telegraphic ribbons of print streamed out of nothing and back into nothing, and animals lived their fivesecond cycles in invisible iron cages, and from tilted bottles poured ceaseless cataracts of bulbs, and the pneumatic nightmare bounced in and out of hiding, and motorcars rode standing still on the treadmill of the world, and lightning struck the same place a thousand times a night, and imbecile spearmint soldiers drilled tirelessly for a chewing gum war, and cluttering the intervening spaces were straw hats, silk stockings, camels, clocks, oranges, and fox terriers.

—'You hungry?' he said.

—'Yes.'

—'What do you feel like eating?'

—'I'm broke.'

—'What do you feel like eating?'

—'Anything.'

—'Come on, then.'

—And afterward we walked west to the docks, and we sat down on a stringpiece and watched the dark slowflowing river. The broad black running mass of water washed the saintvitus reflection of lights in Jersey, and it shattered the steady loops of ferrywindows, and it sucked at the cavities in the tartared teeth of the piers, and jutting from the surface like fractured bones were floating bottles, logy lumber, and drowning crates.

—'Where do you head for next?' he said.

—'I don't know.'

—'You never think about it?'

—'No. I just keep on moving.'

—'There's no special place you want to see?'

—'Places aren't special—they're different, that's all.'

—Past a dark pierhead, a squat tug waddled upstream like a duck, but so slowly that it seemed as if someone were holding it back by its tailfeathers. The haul came into view a moment later; it was a chain of freightcar barges, each of them warped by a curvature of the spine.

I stood up, holding out my hand. 'Thanks for the feed,' I said.

—He stood up too. 'Forget it,' he said.

—'So long.'

—'Take this along with you,' he said, offering me a tendollar bill.

—'I don't want it.'

—'Take it—don't be a fool.'

—'I don't want money.'

—'Take it, I tell you. It'll get you that much closer.'

—'To what?'

—'To wherever you're going.'

—I looked at him for a few seconds, and then I put the money in my pocket and walked away....

❖   ❖   ❖

Platt: ... You didn't give a damn whether she was in the room or out. You wouldn't of missed her if she wasn't, and you just didn't pay her any notice if she was. You couldn't recollect her words five minutes after she'd said them. You wouldn't know what she was wearing even if you took an hour off to fix it in your mind. You couldn't even picture her face once she'd walked out of sight.

But all the same, she set such an almighty store by that measly carcass of hers that you'd of thought it was worth its weight in gold. To listen to her whining day in and day out, you'd figure the end was only a matter of days, and it was nothing short of a miracle how she managed to stand up on her two feet. But God was her rock, she used to say, and He was supporting her because there was such a lot of work to be done—only she never done it. She just didn't have any time to. She was too damn busy groaning and complaining about a pain here and an ache there and a sore spot in every other God damn square inch of her body. No woman in Christ's world could of had so many sicknesses all at one time; if my wife only had one out of every four that she used to name, she'd of died in such terrible agony that folks over in Vermont would of heard her howling.

First of all, she had pleurisy, and that kept her flat on her back about five days a month. Every couple of weeks she'd pop up with an attack of pleurisy that come mighty near to ruining her—maybe. I didn't know what pleurisy was, and I don't think she did, neither, but that didn't stop her and pleurisy calling each other by their first name, and from the way the sickness come back regular as clockwork, you'd think it was by appointment.

Then there was something she used to call varicose veins. It was something about the veins in her legs getting all swole out with standing on her feet all day. She must of done her standing around in bed because for all the use I seen her get out of her legs they could just as well of been sawed off at the knees—but she had varicose veins, and that's all there was about it. The doctoring she put herself through was pretty good to watch; it used to give me ideas about how to get old iron tires off of wagonwheels. When an attack come on, my wife'd soak her legs in water so Godawful hot that you'd of bet the skin was going to peel right off and take the veins along with it. After about an hour of that soaking, she'd mix herself up some kind of a paste, and then she'd rub the stuff in so hard that you'd think she was trying to wear her hand off up to the elbow. After that she'd bring out her wrapping flannel—special for varicose veins—and she'd bandage her legs from the ankles all the way up to the knees. All night long she'd rot inside of them cloths, and by the time morning come around there wasn't anything left of them varicose veins but the stink of the salve.

One of her best things was the hernia, and all she needed to make her think she had it was a pain in the belly, an ordinary little pain like anybody'd have a thousand times in his life. I remember the first time her guts come out of true; her actions had me so buffaloed that I followed her upstairs and peeked through the keyhole. She got undressed down to her corset, and when she'd eased that a bit, she took a stone about the size of your fist and shoved it down in between the corset and the place where she had the pain. Then she trussed herself up tighter than ever, and the whole livelong day she went around with that rock digging at her belly. When we was in bed that night, I just couldn't help feeling my hand about to see what she'd done to herself, and by

God, there was a dent alongside of her navel big enough for a cat to of slept in!

On top of all them regular complains that only come on in certain spells—like the hernia, and pleurisy, and rheumatism, and piles—she had a whole string of plain ones that plagued her every damn day. There was always something the matter with her ears and nose, so she always kept them plugged up with little balls of cotton. I never did find out what she doused on the ones that she rammed up her nose, but every winter she was good for about a gallon of camphorated oil on them rundown ears of hers. The stuff stank up the house worse than a polecat, and it changed the taste of coffee and tobacco and everything else that you put in your mouth, but day after day there was that wife of mine hanging over the stove and brewing up the oil like a witch.

Every time there wasn't any more dangerous sickness for her to be ailing with, she'd take an eyecup and bathe her eyes for hours on end, and that little hunk of glass seen enough use to of wore a hole clean through her face. She was going blind, she used to say, what with all the reading and needlework she had to do. About sewing, I don't think she could of told a needle from a hacksaw, and when it come to reading she'd get plain addlepated trying to give you the right time—but she was going blind.

One of the things that tried her soul pretty near as bad as anything else was gas—just ordinary gas. She'd be setting at the table and eating her head off, and all at once she'd quit right in the middle of a mouthful, and she'd get a gone look in her eyes like she was laying an egg, and then she'd turn loose such a meantempered belch that you'd think you was being snarled at by a God damn wildcat.

But drafts—that was what really kept her hopping like a louse on a griddle! She never once set down anywheres but what she wasn't in a draft. It didn't make any difference what kind of a day it was; the air could be so still that you wouldn't hardly be able to catch your breath, and the sweat could be pouring off of you like rain—but just leave it to that woman to pick out the one spot in the county where the wind was blowing up a regular cyclone. God never made the wind strong enough to bust through all the protection she wore, summer and winter alike, but, by Jesus, to watch her snoop around trying to stop up cracks, you'd think she was laying out naked in the snow!

Oh, she was a beaut, Mrs. Aaron Platt was! To this very day I don't know how I lasted out them five years of marriage. I still wonder sometimes how in hell I kept myself from booting her right off of the property. Lots of times I used to think about doing just that thing, but somehow or other I never got around to it, and finally she saved me the trouble.

It's funny, but all that dosing and pampering she give herself, and all that soaking and wrapping and sweating and gargling and God knows what—it didn't do her one damn bit of good. She put an almighty amount of faith into them remedies and cures she cooked up for herself, but the one thing she forgot was that camphorated oil and kidney pills and mustard plasters and echinacea was a whole lot short of adding up to God.

It's a funny thing the way she finally got took off—she was the one that was always so fidgety about drafts and in the end that's what must of got to her. It was in the middle of spring, almost five years after we got married, that she put herself to bed with a cold. It didn't get any better in the next couple of days, so I called in Doc Slocum. He done what he could, but it wasn't enough to stop the cold turning into pneumonia, and once that laid ahold of her skinny body, it was all up with her. Three more days was all she lasted, and then she died....

⚜ ⚜ ⚜

—... O crawling carnelian
that is in the cleft of the rock,
in the secret places of the stairs,

under the linoleum in the kitchen,
in the horsehair jungle of a mattress—
let me hear thy voice,
for sweet is thy voice,
and let me see thy countenance,
for thy countenance is comely.
Behold, thou art fair, my love;
behold, thou art fair.
Thy hair is as tickertape unfurled
upon a carnival of parading heroes;
thy neck is like a skyscraper tower
builded for an army of peddlers, and
whereon are gilded a thousand trademarks,
all shields of mighty men;
thy lips are sores,
the running purple fires
of a thirdrail in the rain.
I am black, but comely.
Thy teeth are ferryslips and jetties
stained green with rivertartar.
How beautiful are thy feet with bohunk shoes!
Threedollar Perth Amboy shoes!
How beautiful are thy feet with paper shoes!
Not wanting in liquor
is the round goblet of thy navel,
for who that passes the Reservoir
refrains from spitting?
I am black, but comely.
Thy breasts are like twin gas tanks
rigid above a littered acre
in which an old goat is feeding—
feeding not with pleasant fruits,
not among the lilies,
not in an orchard of pomegranates,

not among camphire or spikenard,
but on trampled milkweed
and lastyear's rotogravure.
Behold, thou art fair, my love;
behold, thou art fair ....
—And I thought: *I want this—I want only to know that I shall*
hear no voices, that I shall see no movement, that I shall hear no
invasion of my mobile space in the void. Cut me off from the long
tradition of trespass. Dismiss me from history ....
    5¢ FARE 5¢
my last nickel for a ferryride
on the *Wilkes Barre,*
an old slob of a barge
squatting between the bulkheads
like a fat woman in a bathtub,
her wooden mouth gaping,
her glass eyes staring,
her nostrils clogged with motorcars,
her iron tongue stuck out at Jersey.
Two white screams of steam, and then
motion ....
East: the stone hair of the city—
north: the hard collar of the Palisades—
west: the cemetery of factories—
south: the gangrened arm of America.
But beyond the graveyard
a comber of green,
cumulus over the Schooleys,
the sun in the long afternoon ....
—'Ride ... ?'
—The old seafloor of the Hackensack Meadows,
crawlinground of prehistoric crabs,
huntinground of idiot dreamfish,
burialground of their bone and shell.

The old saltcellar of the Hackensack Meadows,
sunken garden of reeds and cat tail,
sunflowers and dandelions,
slag, tin cans, and decaying scows.
The old seacellar of the Hackensack Meadows,
salt marsh at low tide,
sewer at high,
and over the Plank Road
the heatwaves featherdancing....
—'Ride...? Thanks.'
—'Where you heading?'
—'Straight ahead.'
—'Trenton?'
—'Fine.'
—'Hold on!...'

❧ ❧ ❧

Platt: ... The house she lived in was the last one before the Thurman bridge, and it set out on a little point between the river and the road. It was the neatest place I ever seen in my life, and even when I only wanted to set around and chew the fat with her, it was a pleasure to pay the Widder a call.

The first room you come to was the parlor. The pieces was a good thirty years behind the times, but from the shape they was in, you'd think they'd been kept under glass since the day they was bought. The sofa with its waffled leather, the Morris chair, the red plush armchairs and their fresh doilies, the upright piano, the table and the little clump of china figures that stood on the centerpiece—all of them looked like they'd just come in from the factory. Everything in the room was spotless—the spiral flowerjars, the cigarband ashtrays, the rubberplant that stuck out its long green tongues at you, even the brass spittoon over on the tiles of the fake fireplace.

Right in back of the parlor was the kitchen, and the Widder had it so spic and span that a mouse would of starved to death there before it found so much as a crumb laying around loose. The diningroom was off to one side of the parlor, only it wasn't a diningroom any more; it was a bedroom, and that's where the Widder used to take her customers.

Up above, there was only two rooms, one of them closed off and the other used by the Widder for herself. Along one wall of the Widder's room there was a double bed covered by a spread dotted with hundreds of little candlewicks. Resting on a couple of pairs of pegs in the woodwork was a cavalry saber and a Kragjörgensen rifle. An old sombrero hung off of another peg by its chinstrap, and on either side of this there was a photograph, one of Colonel Teddy Roosevelt dressed up in the uniform of a roughrider, and the other of a cavalry troop lazing around a flatcar in the Tampa yards. A canvas cartridgebelt, spread out like a snakeskin, was tacked up under the hat and the pictures. Over the head of the bed there was a big handpainted photograph of the Widder and her husband in their wedding rig. A little table stood over near the window. On this laid a plush box with a glass cover, and in the box, sunk down in a bed of cotton wadding, was a Medal of Honor.

For a good ten years I don't think I missed a single Saturday afternoon at the Widder's; that was my regular time with her, and she wouldn't even leave anybody else onto the grounds while I was there. I paid her a dollar whether I used her or not, and to show that she wasn't out to make money off of me, she'd pretty near always produce some sandwiches, cakes, and milk along about the time we finished up our other business. She'd serve the feed out on the porch if the weather was nice, and afterwards we'd set there chinning till it got dark.

I used to like that part of the afternoon as much as the rest. A sociable kind of woman, the Widder was, always treating you like you'd just dropped in on her to be neighborly, and it wouldn't be so far from the truth if I said that's just what I done. There wasn't anybody in Warrensburg that'd even talk to me in the road, let alone have me in their house, and so far's I can recollect the Widder was the one and only friend I ever had.

"Aaron," she said to me once, "there's something been on my mind for quite a while."

"What's that, ma'am?" I said.

"It's about you paying me money."

"Ain't it enough, ma'am?"

"Enough! My gosh, man, it's too much!"

"A dollar's too much? How do you figure that out?"

"The way I look at it is I shouldn't be taking any money off of you at all. It's a shame to take money off of your friends."

"You got to live, ma'am."

"All the same, I just wish you wouldn't pay me."

"Say that to a couple of more people, and you'll be over to the Poor Home in no time."

"I don't say it to anybody else. I only say it to you."

She didn't like you bastards any more than I did, and she had plenty of cause too. She was still a mighty pretty girl when they shipped her dead husband back from Cuba, and all of you sonsofbitches seen to it that she paid up good and proper for being pretty. After a while I guess she figured that if you was what's called respectable, it'd be a whole lot more so to go on being a whoor.

"Why, would you believe it, Aaron," she once said, "if I was to tell you that one of them villagers down there—I ain't naming any names—he come in here for something he never in all his days got off of his wife, and then he tried to pass me a Canadian dollar in the dark?"

"Sure I'd believe it," I said.

"Honest to goodness, you'd think a man'd have more self-respect than to do a thing like that."

"Well, knowing some of them as I do down there to Warrensburg, they're so blame tightassed—excuse the expression, ma'am—it's a wonder they don't try to pay off in soap coupons."

"Most people ain't such a much, Aaron," she said, "and I don't only mean the ones around here. I mean everywheres, all over. They're pretty much the same any place—that's what I found out after more than twenty years of doing business with them. Trouble is they don't have any respect, either for themselves or anybody else .... I ever tell you about that little pimpleface man come busting in here once?"

"Pimpleface man? No, I don't think you did."

It was some years back, she said, along about the time Trubee Pell killed that soldier up to his pa's farm. She was in the kitchen baking up a cake when she heard a banging on the screendoor, but figuring it was only one of the customers, she just said, "Be right out, whoever's there. I'm looking after a cake. Set down and take your ease."

After a while she finished her work back there, and then she went to see who it was. This little pimpleface man was laying stretched out in the hammock smoking a cigarette.

"Good afternoon, mister," she said.

He didn't even set up. He said, "I come to see the Widder."

"I'm the Widder."

When she said that, the little pimpleface man shot up so damn fast that the hammock come near skating out from under him. "*You're* the Widder!" he said. "Why, that lying porter over at the Inn said the Widder was so old she held herself together with string!"

"I'm fortyseven."

"Well, by Jesus, you don't look half of that. How you feeling, baby?"

"I guess I'm all right," she said, "only I ain't a baby."

"I don't give a damn what you are! For a hustler, you're a mighty neatlooking piece. Come on over here and get acquainted."

"What's a hustler, mister?" she said.

"A hustler? A hustler's a dame that.... Come on, cutie, quit your kidding. Get alongside of me, and I'll show you a couple of new ones I picked up in Paris."

"Paris! You mean the Paris that's over in Europe across the ocean?"

"Gay Paree, as we say where I come from."

"Paris! Just think of it! You're the first person I ever met that went there. It must of been wonderful, just wonderful!"

"I don't know about it being so hot. Them frogs struck me as being a little on the snotty side. The dames, though—they sure know all the tricks. Many's the soldier stayed over there account of the dames."

"Did you say soldier, mister? You was a soldier in the *army?*"

"You bet your sweet life! One of the best soldiers in the whole God damn war!"

"I declare, I never heard the like of it. Why, my husband was a soldier too!"

"No kidding."

"You come inside, and I'll show you."

"That's where I wanted to go in the first place."

He followed her in the parlor, and he stood there in the middle of the room, shaking his head. "Say," he said, "this is one highclass dump!"

"There on the piano—that's my husband's picture."

He went over closer to look at it. "So that's the soldier boy."

"Yes, mister. That's my husband."

"Funnylooking bird," he said. "Looks like Desperate Desmond with them hairy wings sprouting out from under his bugle."

"I don't think he's funnylooking. People used to say he was a wellmade man."

"What in hell was he—a roughrider?"

"Yes, mister. He was with Teddy Roosevelt."

"Look at the uniform! Them pants is about six sizes too big for him. They could of shoved a soldier down each leg—then there'd of been a war, by God!"

"That's the kind of a uniform they had in them days."

"Look at the way he's standing, with his chin stuck out and his dome screwed around like Roosevelt come along and said he wanted to take a squint down his left ear! And what's he got one of his legs pushed out in front of him for? You'd think he was going into a dance any minute. And the hat cast an eye on the hat! He's got it draped back across his arm like it was a bouquet of flowers."

"Times change, mister. I used to think he looked kind of elegant in that uniform—still do, as a matter of fact."

"He don't look like no fighter to me. He looks more like a Polack bridegroom."

"He was a sergeant."

"A top kick. You don't tell!"

"Yes, and he got killed in a battle."

"What with—a fountainpen?"

"He got shot with a dumdum bullet."

"He must of been loading his gun."

"No, it didn't happen like that. He went out to bring back a captain that was shot in the leg and couldn't walk. He went out in the fields where the captain was laying, and he picked up the captain and took him back even though the Spanish was shooting off their guns at him all the time."

"He must of did that in the middle of the night."

"It was in the morning. Just as he come back with the captain, the Spanish shot him in the spine with a dumdum bullet. Poor man, he died a little while after in the hospital. First, though, he got the Medal of Honor for what he done. I guess you got a medal too."

"I got four," the pimpleface man said, "only some louse went and crooked them off of me."

"That's too bad."

"Say, listen—did we come in here to talk about medals or what? Let's go upstairs."

"What do you figure on doing there?"

"This what you're stalling for?" the pimpleface man said, pulling a dollar bill out of his pocket. "Now, where's the bedroom?"

"Up above. Where'd you think it was?"

"Let's go, then."

"But what do you want to do up there?"

"I'm sick and tired of this playing around. I come here on business, and I don't want nobody making out I'm just one of the neighbors trying to loan some flour. Here's your dollar. Let's get on up to the bedroom."

"I don't know what you're aiming to do, mister, but if you got your heart set on having a look at the bedroom, I guess it ain't too much bother showing it to you."

She went in first, and he come after.

"Cozy," he said, and he give her a shove.

She lost her balance and fell flat on her back over the candlewick spread. He tore out of his coat, flopped down on top of her, and began kissing her all over the face and neck. She tried not to cry, but she couldn't help it, and he got mad.

"Save your bawling for some softhearted yokel!" he said. "What the hell *is* this—a funeral?"

"You don't know what I'm crying about."

"And I don't give a damn! I come here on business."

"This room's mine and my husband's. I never done anything up here."

"Then what did you bring me for?"

"I thought you wanted to see the house."

"*See the house!* God damn it, I got a good mind to slug you one! I come here on business, and it's business I'm going to do."

Saying that, he dove at her again. His arm hit something on the table and knocked it onto the floor, breaking something made out of glass.

"What was that?" the woman said.

"How the hell do I know? Give us a kiss."

"What fell down?"

"Make believe you love me, baby."

"*What fell down?*"

"That God damn box! Let it lay!"

"The box! The box with the medal! Get up off of me!"

"Kiss me on the mouth. Come on."

She worked her hands under his chest and heaved him off of the bed. She picked up the medal.

The little pimpleface man looked up from the floor. "What's the big idea?" he said.

The Widder was busy polishing the medal with the skirt of her dress.

The little pimpleface man stood up. "That's a hell of a way to treat customers," he said, and then for the third time he sailed into the woman.

She tried to fend him off, but he dodged around her arm and caught it under his own, and with his back to her he started putting on some kind of a wrassling hold. She just lifted her foot and put it against the seat of his pants, and the next thing he knew he was laying all coiled up in a corner.

"Clear out, mister," she said.

"What do you mean—clear out? I come here on business, and my dough's as good as the next man's."

"Your money's all right, but I can't say I cotton to your ways. You don't have any respect, so I'll have to ask you to clear out."

"Clear out, hell! I don't quit this dump till I get what I come here for."

The Widder got up off of the bed. "If you don't show me a clean pair of heels by the time I count three, I'm going to pitch you down them stairs."

"Pitch *who* down *what* stairs, you old bum?"

"One … ," she said.

"Come on, now. Don't be sore at little Jimmy."

"Two … ," she said.

"Please! Tell you what—I'll give you *two* bucks. How's that strike you?"

"Three … ," she said, and she started for him.

"Ah, *please!*" he said, backing out the doorway.

She whipped out and caught ahold of the sleeve of his shirt. He got free, though, and flew down the stairs, taking the last four on the jump. She chucked his coat down after him ….

"People ain't such a much, Aaron," she always used to say ….

❧   ❧   ❧

—… And there, with half the country before me and half at my back, with my feet in the sluggish drainage of the continental ileum and touching for the first time the putrefactive slime of history, I knew why I had always liked abandoned things. The discarded clothes, the deserted houses, the broken machinery, the overgrown roads—no one would ever envy me my possession of them, no one would dispute my claim, no one would kill me to add them to his estate. They were immune to trespass ….

—… '*I feel*,'

wrote General Terry to General Sheridan,

'*that our plan must have been successful*

had it been carried out,

and I desire you to know the facts ….

In the action itself,

so far as I can make out,
Custer acted under a misapprehension.
He thought, I am confident,
that the Indians were running.
For fear that they might get away,
he attacked without getting all his men up
and divided his command
so that they were beaten in detail ...'
No, the Indians were not running.
Flintlock, blunderbuss, and carbine
had run them for three hundred years,
from the Chesapeake flats,
from the Catskill highlands,
from the dunes of Kitty Hawk,
from the Okeechobee swamps,
and then cannonballs and promises
had ferried them to the plains,
and then Gold—
and their backs were to the wall.
But there were still some medals
that Custer had not won,
and there were still some commissions
that he had not earned,
and the Sioux were the only enemy
the white man had on the continent,
the only enemy to take the field,
the only enemy to be killed
for those medals and commissions—
and Custer knew that.
But the Indians were not running.
They had run two thousand miles
to escape the stick that spoke,
but for once they too had Winchesters
(never mind where they got them),

and Gall and Two Moon and Crazy Horse
were making their last stand—
and Custer didn't know that.
And when the last shot was fired,
when the smoke had cleared away,
when the Indians were gone,
and the sun was going down,
Custer stank as he rotted
among other rotting corpses
on the upshot ground
of the valley of the Little Big Horn.
All books speak of his curly yellow hair,
but how looked that hair
about his negroid sunken mask of death?
and that fringed buckskin jacket
that he wears in the beerhall prints,
how romantic was it
with its sprays of drydark blood?
and how eloquent were the dusty revolvers
and the broken blade?
and what song was droned by bottleflies
as they played in the heatwaves
above the stiffened body?
'I feel,' wrote General Terry,
'that our plan must have been successful had it
been carried out,
and I desire you to know the facts....'
But the facts were gone,
like the medals and commissions,
like Custer's blood,
and they were draining through the earth
to fill the open sewer of America,
and the facts are here
in the roots of trees,

in the smooth silt,
in the mud ....
—... *'They are naturally inclined to Drink,'*
wrote Governor Dinwiddie,
'and they are a very awkward,
dirty fett of People,
yet abfolutely neceffary
to attack the Enemy's Indians
in their way of fighting
and fcowering the Woods before an Army.
I am perfwaded they will appear
a defpicable fett of People
to his Lordfhip and you
but they will expect
to be taken particular Notice of,
and now and then fome few Prefents.
It will be a prudent ftepp
to reftrain them with Moderation,
and by fome of your fubalterns
to fhew them Refpect.
I fear General Braddock
defpifed them too much.
which probably was of Diftervice to him ....
It was only a holiday for Braddock,
that Pennsylvania campaign,
but he's there yet
because of his contempt for
a very awkward, dirty fett of People.
Contrecœur, commanding Fort Duquesne,
did not despise them.
He sent out six hundred under Beaujeu
to sit in the forest
and wait for the redcoats
to make an autumn in June,

and when they did,
from behind fallen trees,
from behind corroded rocks,
from among the spinning leaves,
a very awkward, dirty fett of People
mowed them down,
and on the rough new road
lay a harvest of British
and some few provincials
that had not had time
to find an ambush of their own.
The provincials knew
what Braddock refused to know,
that if you wanted to live
you fought the Indians
as they fought you—
from behind fallen trees,
from behind corroded rocks,
from among the spinning leaves—
and so they took to cover, the provincials,
and covered, returned the Indians' fire.
This went against Braddock's grain.
He was a soldier, you understand,
and when you had a rifle in your hands,
you behaved like a soldier;
you stood on your feet in the open,
like a soldier,
like a God damn man,
and let the enemy pop away
until they brought you down
or ran out of shot;
only a savage fired a gun
while lying on his belly,
and, by Christ, there were no savages

in Braddock's command!
He gave the order for the provincials
to come back into the road,
and when one of them was slow to obey,
he buried his sword in the coward's skull
to show the other craven dogs
that Braddock was a very brave man. But many brave men
had waded with him through Turtle Creek,
and one of them
(Faucett, they say his name was,
a brother of the man struck down)
was standing behind Braddock
when the blow fell—
and that went against *his* grain.
He raised his rifle
and sighted down the fivefoot barrel
as if at a chunk of bark under a coon,
and then he let the brave General
have a sinker of lead square in the back,
blowing him to hell out of his saddle
and pitching him into the bloodwet dirt.
'Now watch these fancy bastards run!'
Faucett must have said,
and run they did from
a very awkward, dirty sett of People.
There was still some life in Braddock,
so they picked him up and dragged him along
as they fled to escape an enemy
they had yet to see,
and with them went this Faucett
(or Fawcett, or Fossit, or whatever it was—
nobody seemed to know exactly),
and again they forded Turtle Creek,
this time flinging away

everything that would check their flight—
guns, belts, food, even gold—
everything but Braddock,
and before long
they had to get rid of him too
because he died.
They buried him in their own road,
and then fearing that
a very awkward, dirty fett of People
would find the body,
they marched their whole army
over the newturned ground
to wipe out traces of the grave.
They did a good job,
for only one man remembered
where it was.
His name was Faucett
(or Fawcett, or was it Fossit?)....
A gang of workmen were digging culverts
under an old road,
and one of them looked up and saw
an old man sitting on a rock,
a man older than the road,
and the man smiled and said,
'If you would find a prize,
dig there where that yellow leaf
has fallen upon that stone.'
And being poor, and being men,
they fell to tearing at the ground,
and the yellow leaf and the stone
were in the first spadeful
to be tossed away.
The old man picked up the leaf
and spun it in his fingers,

remembering.
The workmen found not gold in the road,
but a skeleton,
and they were angered.
'Is this your prize?' they asked,
and the old man answered, 'Yes.'
And one of them, being curious, said,
'How did you know that
these bones were buried here?'
'Tell me,' the old man said,
'has the skeleton a broken spine?'
'And if it has?' the curious one said.
The old man played with the leaf,
remembering. 'If it has,' he said,
'you are kneedeep in history.
That spine is General Braddock's.'
'Braddock! Braddock the Englishman!
But it must be seventy years now...!'
'The spine is broken,'
one of the workmen said.
The old man laughed and walked away,
leaving the workmen standing in the road.
They thought he was crazy....
And British blood too is in the earth,
seeping down the cracks
between the grains of sand
to fill the open sewer of America,
and the blood is here
in the roots of trees,
in the smooth silt,
in the mud....
—... ANSWER (by Major Anthony):
There was one little child,
probably three years old,

just big enough to walk through the sand.
The Indians had gone ahead,
and this little fellow, perfectly naked,
was following after them.
I saw one man get off his horse,
at a distance of about seventy-five yards,
and draw up his rifle and fire:
he missed the child.
Another man came up and said,
"Let me try the sonofabitch;
I can hit him."
He got down off his horse, kneeled,
and fired at the little child,
but he missed him.
A third man came up
and made a similar remark, and fired,
and the little fellow dropped.'
QUESTION: *'Those were men of your command?'*
ANSWER: *'Of Colonel Chivington's....'*
There were no Confederates to be killed
in that part of the Union
(that was being taken care of in Georgia
at Kennesaw Mountain and Chickamauga),
and blue uniforms were wearing out
at the seat,
and brandnew Sharps rifles
were going out of fashion,
and soldiers were getting restless,
fearing that the war would be over
before they could let some blood
to irrigate the plains.
And then they remembered,
as always when their fingers itched,
the Indian.

They remembered that he too had blood,
just like any white man;
that he too caved in like empty clothes
when he had a bullet in his lung;
that he too dug his nails into the ground
for a little while
and then lay still,
just like any white man—
and anyhow the Indian was fair game,
for it was a matter of common knowledge
that the only good one was a dead one.
Having no real enemy to try their guts,
the Federals invented one.
A thousand cavalry took to horse
to scour the plains for hostiles,
and just to make the fight an even one,
just to be on the safe side in case
the Cheyennes had artillery of their own,
four cannon went with their train.
They rode like hell for a long time
without sighting a single hostile,
without flushing an Indian of any kind,
and after a hard week of drinking
(anything wrong with whisky, mister?),
it began to dawn on Chivington
that if they were too damn choosy
about the disposition of the Indians,
the liquor was apt to run out
before smoke was smelled.
After all, it was common knowledge that
the only good Indian was a dead Indian,
so why make any bones about whether
he was a hostile or a friend?
Christ, *any* Indian would bite the dust!

'Look,' Chivington told the boys,
'I know where we can get three shots
for a lot less than a nickel.
Remember Black Kettle's Cheyennes,
the ones that come to me back in Denver,
telling how friendly they was to us whites?
Well, I give 'em a couple of flags,
a white one and an American,
and sent 'em off up to Sand Creek,
saying if they ever ran afoul of troops
they should hist up the colors
and then the white surrender flag,
and they'd be took good care of.
What I say is, a promise is a promise.
Sand Creek ain't so far away ....'
Far! They'd have made it in an hour
if it weren't for the damn guncarriages!
As it was, it took them all night long.
Five suns rose that morning—
one from the hills and four from cannon—
and the sleeping band of Cheyennes
were blown awake and limb from limb.
The hotbloods made a show of fight,
got out their defective oneshot rifles,
and tried to bag cannonballs in midair—
but not Black Kettle, the white man's friend,
the brave who owned an American flag
(red for the Indian, white for the paleface,
and blue for a cloudless sky over both),
not Black Kettle!
Still believing, he took Chivington's gifts,
ran them up to the top of his lodge,
and waited for the firing to cease,
for the soldiers to realize their mistake,

but through all that smoke and alcohol
God only knows what flag they saw—
the English, maybe, the cross of St. George—
and the soldiers remained in error
for a good four hundred minutes,
letting the blood of two hundred Cheyennes
(Two minutes an Indian? Bad shootin', boys!).
Black Kettle blackcursed the day
God made white meat and caused it to multiply,
and he backed slowly away from Sand Creek,
firing.
The troops came on to finish the job,
and according to one of their own officers,
they did it well:
'In going over the battle-ground the next day,
I did not see a body of man, woman, or child
but was scalped;
I heard one man say that
he had cut a woman's private parts out
and had them for exhibition on a stick;
I heard another man say that
he had cut the fingers off of an Indian
to get the rings on the hand;
I heard one instance of a child
a few months old
being thrown in the feed-box of a wagon,
and after being carried some distance,
left on the ground to perish;
I also heard of numerous instances
in which men had cut out
the private parts of females,
and stretched them over the saddle-bows,
and wore them over their hats,
while riding in the ranks.

According to the best of my knowledge
these atrocities that were committed
were with the knowledge of J. M. Chivington,
and I did not know of his taking any measures
to prevent them ....'
And so Indian blood too is in the earth,
helping the feeble run of Sand Creek
to fill the open sewer of America,
and the blood is here
in the roots of trees,
in the smooth silt,
in the mud ....
—... He was with Pizarro in Peru
as captain of a troop of horse—
where else could a nobody
(with nothing but blade and buckler)
have put together as his share of the loot
two hundred thousand cruzados in gold?
where else could a nobody
(with nothing but avarice and cruelty)
have plundered enough to obtain
a superintendent of household,
an usher, an equerry, and a chamberlain,
and pages, footmen, and other servants
requisite for the menage of a gentleman?
where else could a nobody
(with nothing at all)
have slaughtered his way to such renown
that he could claim the hand of a
Doña Ysabel de Bobadilla
and cause the Emperor to make him
Governor of the island of Cuba
and Adelantado of Florida,
with the title of Marquis for good measure?

where but in Peru? ...
When, therefore, one Cabeza de Vaca,
who had been in Florida with Narváez,
arrived at Court with tales of gold
that sprouted up from the earth like mustard,
that tumbled in the water like old leaves,
that grew on trees like Seville oranges,
who will wonder that such ravings
made de Soto forget his superintendent
and his ushers and footmen and chamberlain
and all the other servants
requisite for the menage of a gentleman,
forget even his Doña Ysabel de Bobadilla? ...
They had a letter from him once only
after he had refitted and sailed from Havana.
'Very Noble Gentlemen,' he wrote:
'At my arrival here I received news
of there being a Christian
in the possession of a Cacique,
and I sent Baltazar de Gallegos,
with XL men of the horse,
and as many of the foot,
to endeavor to get him.
They found the man
a day's journey from this place,
with eight or ten Indians,
whom he brought into my power.
We rejoiced no little over him,
for he speaks the language;
and although he had forgotten his own,
it directly returned to him.
His name is Juan Ortiz, an hidalgo,
native of Sevilla ... .'
And again Gallegos was sent into the land,

now with lancers and infantry
to the number of one hundred and eighty,
and the land was found to be good.
There were vast fields of maize, he wrote,
and beans, and pumpkins, and other fruits,
and there were provisions in such quantity
as would suffice to subsist an army
without its ever knowing a want,
and there was another town, Ocale by name,
a town so large and so extolled that
he hardly dared repeat what was said of it,
but could there be any harm in his telling
of the great plenty to be found there,
of the multitude of turkeys kept in pens,
of the herds of tame deer that were tended
as a Spanish peasant tended his cattle,
of the many trades among the Ocale people,
of the intercourse with neighboring towns,
and, lastly, of the striking abundance
of gold and silver and many pearls? ...
And so when de Soto's men (and de Soto)
went each night to their damascene dreams,
they dreamed not of fig trees
that bore fruit as big as the fist;
nor of another tree called the anane,
which was in the shape of a small pineapple,
and whereof the pulp seemed to be a curd;
nor of still another tree called the mamei,
more than any esteemed by the people,
for it yielded a fruit as tender as a peach;
nor did they dream of the guayaba,
which is formed in the likeness of a filbert;
nor of the strangest tree of all,
which is merely a stalk without any branch,

and of which the fruit is like a cucumber,
the bunch having twenty or thirty of these,
and called by the people plantanos;
nor did they dream of the nourishing batata
which grew in profusion everywhere,
recalling the taste of the chestnut
and yet looking like the ynhame;
nor of the humpbacked cows did they dream;
nor the wild hogs and swiftleaping conies;
nor the many varieties of living things
that were to be found in the water,
such as the bagre, a third of which was head,
and the one that was like the barbel,
and the other that was like the bream
save for a head rightful to the hake,
and the peelfish, with a snout a cubit long
and an upper lip shaped like a shovel,
and the shad, which was full of scale,
and the pereo, which had rows of teeth
above and below ....
There was much gold in that new land,
and in all truth, even as de Vaca had said,
it sprouted up from the earth like mustard,
and it tumbled in the water like old leaves,
and it grew on the trees like Seville oranges,
but de Soto and his men saw not this gold,
for they were hunting another kind,
a gold that weighed heavy in the hand,
a gold that shone in the light,
a gold that would ornament their persons
and be sounding when struck.
And so they wandered for three years,
killing every living thing, and being killed,
killing for as little as an unopened oyster

that might contain a pearl,
but never did they find de Vaca's gold
that weighed heavy in the hand and shone,
and at last they came upon a flow of water
so great that it tore trees from the earth
and then tore away the earth itself,
and beyond this water, south and north,
they saw more of the inexhaustible jungle.
And it was then that the Adelantado
knew that they would never find
what they had pawned their lives for,
and being sick of a fever,
he took to his pallet and died,
and his men (what was left of them)
wrapped his body in blankets
and weighted the blankets
not with gold and silver, but sand,
and sank it in the stream ....
And so Spanish blood too
is in the open sewer of America,
and the blood is here
in the roots of trees,
in the smooth silt,
in the mud ....
—... *I want this—I want only to know that I shall hear no voices,
that I shall see no movement, that I shall fear no invasion of my
mobile space in the void. Cut me off from the long tradition of
trespass. Dismiss me from history ....*

❖ ❖ ❖

Platt: ... "People ain't such a much, Aaron," she always used
to say. "People ain't such a much."

Nobody's got a good memory when it comes to things that don't exactly show him off in his best light, so I guess there wouldn't be a one of you can recall that Saturday about five years ago when I drove through the town on my way to the Widder's. If I was to ask you about it, you'd look off somewheres in the top of a tree and say, "Seems to me like you went out there *every* Saturday, didn't you?"

But there was one particular Saturday that you'd make out you just couldn't remember no matter how hard you tried. The day I mean was the day I come up the road in my wagon the same as I always done. There was something different about Warrensburg, though. There wasn't only the regular four or five out in front of Polk's store; I counted a couple of dozen. And people just wasn't going about their business, either; they looked like they was waiting for something, and from the way they gawked the minute I got in sight, they looked like they was waiting for *me.* There wasn't a sound as I drove up the pike, only the wheels scratching sand on the pavement, and nobody so much as made a move except to throw open a window or come out of a door.

I didn't think much about it at the time; I set your bad manners down to the fact that I had a kitten in my pocket that I was taking over to the Widder as a present. I'd found the little beast in my barn that morning, and I'd of drowned it only for it being kind of pretty, and I figured maybe the Widder would like to have it around as a pet. Its head was sticking out of my pocket, and it was blinking its eyes in the sunshine; and guessing that you was all rubbering at the kitten more than you was at me, I put you out of my mind and kept on driving.

I didn't want the Widder to hear me coming up, so I left the wagon out by the road and sneaked across the lawn to the porch. I tiptoed up the steps and set the kitten down right inside of the door, and then I give it a little pat on the ass to make it start for the kitchen. It went a ways in the house, and all of a sudden its fur raised up like the spikes onto a porcupine, and back it come towards the door like it was running away from hell. I caught it by the tail as it went by me, and I made another try at getting it to go through the house. There was nothing doing, though; that time the kitten wouldn't even budge. I picked it up and went in.

Right in the middle of the parlor, setting on a couple of saw-horses, was a fivedollar coffin. There was some pencilwritings on one of the planks.

"*She died yesterday,*" the writing said. "*One of the boys found her when he come around to pay a little call. The coffan did not cost any thing we found it in the seller. All you have to do is berry her. We are levying her for you to berry seeing your her best friend.*"

"People ain't such a much," she always used to say ....

☙ ☙ ☙

—... All afternoon I sat on the rocks, watching an offshore wind help the outgoing tide. The run through the Gate was an endless belt of washboard ripples, carrying here and there a meringue of foam toward the Farallones. All afternoon the sea had fled the earth, and now the sun was going down, and still the corrugated water rode out from under me. This was land's end, and the sun was going down, and I was cold.

—No one would give me a ride to the city, so I started across the sandhills toward the coral glare that stained the belly of the mist. It was still far off when my feet began to drag, and I knew that I'd never be able to make the town without a little sleep. There was a single house on a street that had been cut through the dunes, and in the dunes the street ended, the asphalt disappearing into a bank of sand. The house was vacant, and the door to the vestibule open. I lay down on the floortiles.

—Sleep, the warm breeze of sleep, was beginning to roll over me when I felt something clawing at my sleeve. I reached out, and my hand felt the damp fur of a kitten. It was cold, and for a long time after it had crept inside my coat I could feel it trembling. I lay there in the dark, and as I stroked the little animal to sleep, I remembered a story that Nate had told me years before, many years before ....

—... 'Old Amram Platt,' Nate had said, 'his wife died a couple of months ago, and even with Aaron being there to help him out, he's so shorthanded around the farm that he takes me on for a dollar a week and found. I go in his woodshed one morning, and what do I find but a couple of kittens? One's a she, gray all over like iron, and the other, the tom, he's dead white except for one big black patch all around his left eye, making him look like he's got the damnedest shiner you ever did see. I hunt for the mother cat, but I don't turn her up no place, so I figure she's lit out for keeps.

—'Now, I like kittens as much as the next man, but I see where I'm in for the worry of feeding them by hand, and to tell the truth I don't have the time for it, what with the way old Amram Platt works a man, so I make up my mind I'm going to drown the kittens and save them a bellyful of grief, thinking as I do that Platt'll only kick them to hell and gone when he finds out what's been wished on him.

—'I drop the kittens in a bucket, and I'm heading for the pump when along comes the old man, saying, "What's that you got in there, Nate?"

—'I say, "Couple of kittens."

' "Where'd you get them?"

—' "Over in the woodshed."

—' "And what're you going to do with them?"

—' "Drown them," I say.

—'By God, he lets out a bullroar at that. "Drown them!" he says. "Like hell you are!" He sticks his hand down in the bucket and pulls out the kittens. "Maybe when they grow up they could take care of the mice around here."

—'I'm pretty near floored by all this because I never seen that lowlife come in reach of a beast but what he wasn't doing his best to whale the gizzard out of it. This trash about raising the kittens to be mousers, it don't take me in none; the place is simply lousy with mice and rats and all manner of crawling and leaping vermin, and there's no two cats this side of hell can clean it out. The way I look at it is, Platt just takes a plain shine to them kittens because they're so pretty. Of course, if I have my say I don't leave nothing to that mean heart of his; I drown the kittens before he gets sick and tired of them lapping up milk and wrings their little necks for them. The fact is, though, that I don't have no say, so I leave them there with him and get back to work.

—'Suppertime that night, just try and figure out what Mister Amram Platt does before he sets him down to eat. I'm a liar if he don't warm up some milk in a skillet and feed it to the kittens out of a spoon! It takes him quite a while to get enough down to keep them alive, and by the time he's done, his supper's laying there rockhard and cold. You think he lets out a bellow, like he always does when something frets him? Not old man Platt! He eats the food the way it is, by God, and he don't make one single complain!

—'Now, I know all about his character of being a hard one to get along with, and it'd be a waste of time telling me he don't have a living soul he can call his friend, but all the same, when I happen onto somebody of his stamp fiddling around with a couple of kittens just like they're babies, then I have to say that maybe there's something about people that takes a whole lot of finding out.

—'The next few weeks that's just the way Platt does treat the kittens—like babies. The mother cat never comes back, and Platt has to do the feeding himself. They don't touch nothing but what *he* gives them, and even after he learns them how to lick the milk up out of a bowl, they're so used to him being about when they eat that he has to stay in the same room or else they go snooping and sniffing till they smell him out—and make believe that don't tickle Platt silly!

—'I owned plenty of kittens in my time, but never before do I see any chasing a man around like dogs. Many a morning I'm out in the fields with Platt, and they come trailing him to his work, begging him with little noises and rubbing alongside of his boots to catch his eye, and finally he has to pick them up and stuff them in the back pocket of his overhalls, and there they stay, sticking their heads out and blinking at the world till he finds a minute to scoot back to the house and get them some milk to start the day off with.

—'The only thing worries my head is I can't understand his turnabout, and that's why I don't tell nobody when I come over to town on Saturday nights. I just can't picture me saying, "A change is come over Amram Platt account of a couple of kittens." Everybody knows the kind of wood he's made of, I figure, and I don't expect to hardly find a straight face when I say that maybe they all made a mistake about him.

—'One day when the kittens is about eightnine weeks old, I go in the kitchen to get something, and there's Platt holding a kitten by the scruff in either hand. When he hears me, he right away drops them, and out he goes without saying a word, but I see his face as he passes me by, and I want to tell you it sure has one mighty queer look onto it. I'm stumped by that look because I never seen nothing to match it anywheres.

—'Now, I'm wondering what Platt's been doing in there with the kittens, the reason being that it's the first time they ever act like they're ascared of him, and they beat it under the stove when he lets them fall. I poke them out of there and give them a going over, but all I find is a wet spot on the belly of the she. I can't see what that's got to do with Platt, so I forget about it.

—'I'm in the barn later in the day, and when I go over to dump some oats in one of the feedboxes, what do I come across but the little she giving suck to the tom. Of course, she don't have no milk, but that don't stop her trying to give it or the tom trying to get it, and there he lays, shuteyed, working his mouth away like a baby pulling on an empty bottle. I seen that happen before with kittens out of the same litter, and it always give me a laugh.

—'Platt and me and Aaron, that night we're setting around after supper, and the kittens get busy playing wet nurse right in front of us on the floor. Something makes me take a look at the old man, and, by God, his mouth is flattened out to no more than a crease, and his nose is flaring like an umberella, and finally he grabs up a coffeecan and lets fly at the kittens, and they dust to hell out of the room. I ask him what's his idea of pitching the can at the kittens, but he's so full of fury that all he can do is give me a look that's got teeth into it. Aaron don't do nothing; he just sets there.

—'Next night—that's *last* night—the kittens pull off the same stunt, and this time the old man's watching for it. He goes over to where they're laying and boots them clear across the room. The she smacks plank up against the wall, and when she falls down on the floor she lays there like a dead one. The tom lands onto a corner of the woodbox and rips one of his paws open. Aaron still don't do nothing; he just keeps on setting there.

—'I jump up and say I got a good mind to bowl the old man over and mush his face in, and the only thing stops me is he must be a little touched in the head, but loony or no loony, I tell him, if he ever makes another move like that one I'm going to go get me a hayfork and lose it in the back of his pants, handle and all.

—'Platt's just as hot as me, and he wants to know since when am I telling him how to run his farm. "Them kittens belong to me," he hollers, "and no God damn hired man gives me a argument about them!"

—'I say right to his face, "I think a hell of a sight more of them kittens than what I do about your lousy job, you old shitepoke, and if you give me what's owing I'll get my stuff and clear out. I'll be glad to be quits with you, anyway, because even a man with half an eye could see you're still the same blackhearted lowlife that everybody's got you figured out to be."

—' "You'll get your money in the morning," Platt said, "and you can go plumb to hell!"

—'He goes outside after that, and I get busy fixing up the kittens. The she comes around after a couple of minutes, but I have to soak the tom's leg in cold water and then put a bandage onto it because the cut's still bleeding. I watch him try to shake the bandage off and walk at the same time, and I feel bad when he finally has to hobble about on three legs. And all that time Aaron don't do or say a thing; he just sets where he is, staring at the ceiling.

—'This morning's the finish. I'm up above, packing my stuff, and all of a sudden I hear a blast go off. I tear downstairs to see what's a matter, and there's old man Platt out in the yard with a shotgun in his hands, and not far away the kittens is rolling around in the grass pretty near blowed out of their fur. They lay still after a couple of seconds, and that's the end of them.

—'I get so God damn hopping mad that I reach me a rock to brain Platt with, but he covers me with the shotgun, saying, "Get gay, and I give you the other barrel square in the bellybutton." Then he pulls some bills out of his pocket and chucks them onto the ground. "There's your money," he says. "You can go if you promise not to make no stink."

—'Well, he's got such a crazy look on his face that there's no telling what he's apt to do next, and anyhow I'm too late to do the kittens any good, so I drop the rock and give Platt my word. He don't take no chances, though, but keeps me covered all the time I'm picking up the money and getting my satchel and even when I'm scooping out a little hole in the dirt to put the kittens in.

—'I'm flattening down the spot afterwards, and I just can't hold myself in from asking him to please *please* tell me what's his idea of shooting the kittens.

—'He says, "What belongs to me ain't allowed to carry on like that...." ' '

—I got up so suddenly that the sleeping kitten tumbled out of my coat and fell to the floor, and for a moment I stood there in the dark vestibule thinking of remembered words: 'What belongs to me ain't allowed to carry on like that.'

—*'What belongs to me ain't allowed to carry on like that!'*

—I grabbed up the kitten and ran.

—The streetlamps went out just as I reached the top of Market Street, and in the long hike down to the Ferry Building all I was able to bum from the earlybirds was the price of a ride across the Bay. At the far side of Oakland I hit the road once more....

—The kitten was almost a cat by the time I dropped off a freight in the Lake George yards and caught an oiltruck heading north. The driver gave me a lift as far as the Schroon River bridge, and the rest of the way I walked. It was late afternoon when I passed Polk's store. Only one man was on the porch, and as I went by he hailed me. It was Nate.

—'Where you been?' he said.

—'Traveling.'

—'I know that; I ain't seen you around. Where you coming from?'

—'Down the line,' I said, starting to move off.

—He let me get a little distance away before saying, 'Where you going now, Tom?'

—I stopped and looked around. 'Home,' I said. 'What makes you ask?'

—'Nothing,' he said.

—I went back to the porch. 'What makes you ask, Nate?'

—'Nothing.'

—I felt a hole opening up wide somewhere behind my belt-buckle. 'Nate,' I said, 'why did you ask me where I was going?'

—'Well, if you're looking for Grace, you won't find her at the old place no more.'

—'Where is she?' I said, and my voice sounded so unusual that I wanted to look about for the person who had spoken the words. 'Where is she?'

—'Anybody'll tell you,' Nate said. 'I'm busy right now.' He turned away and started into the store.

—I grabbed his arm and dragged him back. 'What do you mean—you're too busy? You had plenty of time to call me over and ask a couple of nosy questions. How about answering one?'

—'Ask somebody up in town,' he said, trying to break loose.

—I dropped the cat, and I took him by the lapels and backed him up against a pillar of the porch. 'I want to know where my wife is, Nate,' I said, 'and if you don't tell me, I'm going to break your God damn head on this beam,' and to show him I meant business I banged him once hard enough to start his eyeballs.

—'No need to get sore at *me*, Tom,' he said. 'Grace is living out to that little house on the Thurman pike.'

—'You should've said so right off. Which one?'

—He looked at me.

—'*Which one?*' I said.

—'The last one.'

—'You lying sonofabitch!' I said, and I let him have a hard one flush on the mouth.

—He didn't even put up his hands; he just stood there.

—'You lying sonofabitch!' I said. 'The last house is the Widder's!'

—Nate nodded....

⚜ ⚜ ⚜

Platt:...I was there when Nate come around and told her what he knew.

"... And when it finally sunk in where you was living, ma'am, all he done was pick up his cat and start back in the same direction he come from."

"Did he say anything, Nate?" Grace said.

"Not right then, ma'am. He just walked off."

"Why didn't you try to stop him?"

"I did try," Nate said. "I run down the road after him, saying he was doing the wrong thing, and if he went away without seeing you he'd regret it all the rest of his life, but he only got sore and said I should mind my own God damn business. I kept on arguing with him till we got down to the bridge, and there all of a sudden he stopped and looked me in the eye. 'If you ever see her,' he said, 'say that what belongs to me ain't allowed to carry on like that.'"

"And that was all, Nate?"

"Yes, ma'am. He closed up tight and wouldn't say another word, and when a car come along he hailed it for a lift. I tried to stop him getting in, but he shook me off. I'm sorry, ma'am. I done the best I could for you."

"That's all right, Nate."

"There anything you want me to do, maybe?"

"No."

"Then I guess I'll be getting back to town," he said, and he started across the lawn.

"Thanks for what you did, Nate," Grace said.

He didn't answer; he just waved and kept on walking....

That was five years ago, and up to this morning she was still waiting for Mister Tom Paulhan to forgive her and come back home. I know what I'm talking about because fiftytwo Saturdays a year I went out to her place with a dollar bill in my hands, but somehow or other I just couldn't ever make myself use it on her. Instead, many's the time I ast her to see a lawyer and get rid of Paulhan so's she could marry me, and always she give me the same answer: "He'll come home, Aaron. Some day he'll come home...."

❧ ❧ ❧

—... And then I remembered that I'd seen it there a few days before. It wasn't healing. It was larger now, and the edges were encrusted, and from the center oozed a flow of sulphur gum that hardened in the air and scaled off. I couldn't understand why there was no pain.

—A druggist told me about a salve that'd dry it up, but it didn't work, so I went around to a clinic. The doctor took a test tube of blood from a vein in my elbow and told me to come back in a week for a report. When I did, he showed me into a small room in which there was nothing but an examination table and a nickel cabinet. He made me sit down on the table and roll up my sleeve, and then he went to the cabinet and fiddled with a hypodermic syringe. He came back and shoved the needle into my arm.

—He told me to come back for a shot every day. 'You've got it,' he said ....

—... and on the stairs the canter of heels, and she went out toward the middle of the floor, not walking, not just walking, but flowing like a comber, and the spotlight flowed with her over the boards, washing across her feet and marooning her on a drifting island, and the crowd came up like a wave breaking on rocks— and then the writhing spiral music, wrapping itself around .... a pout of flesh that he pinched up from my forearm, and I heard the rubbery puncture not with my ears, but my blood, and he shot the plunger down a little too fast, the jet of liquid cysting under the skin .... and slowly she began to flirt the carnation of her dress, a dozen kneehigh skirts amberswirling, and she .... played with the floating plate of light, flashing over it so fast that her skirts came to a boil, chattering the wooden shells until they stuttered like drumfire, now and then stamping her heels so hard that long gray combs of dust sprang from between the floorboards .... and very slow now, the music was, gnashing, and I sat there watching the woman and wiping my palms on the tablecloth, over and over again slowly wiping them on the tablecloth, and then the music slashed up to one last tearing jerking tincan smash, the woman's body cakewalking in the final orgasms of a mechanical jigger

*running down…. and she said, 'He ask me now all the time to
let him be my husband, but I will not do that because then he
will be absolve, and he will forget the thing he do with me when
I am only eleven years old. All his lifetime he will follow me—to
Paris, to Roma, to Nev York, everywhere—and all his lifetime he
will ask me to let him be my husband, even if my belly is fat like
a clown with the child that is not his child, even if I am sick with
the syphilis sickness, even if I am a dirty wrinkled old woman
that has not a good smell in her mouth and between her legs, but
I will never in my lifetime do what he ask. He is now only a good
customer.…' I heard the sound of silk rubbing on silk, of silk being
bunched and thrown away, of silk hushing itself into silence as it
slid along the floor, and feeling the shape of her body through the
back of my coat, I tried my best to think of that little bump on my
arm, but she pressed closer and closer to me, and finally I couldn't
stand it any more, I couldn't stand it any more, I couldn't stand it,
and I had to turn around….*

❧ ❧ ❧

There was no snow during the fifth night, and the next day was
clear but very cold. Platt sat before the stove in the kitchen until
the middle of the morning, and then he set out through the snow
toward his mailbox at the state road. On the way, just beyond a
fieldstone fence that marked the end of his property, he found
Paulhan lying facedown in a drift and frozen hard.

The nearest telephone was at Bertrand's house, halfway to
the village. Platt left the body where it lay and plowed on through
the chokedup road, bucking a fast flat wind for almost an hour
to cover the two miles to Bertrand's. From there he called Sheriff
Smead at Warrensburg.

Smead was on his way in a cutter five minutes after receiving
the call. He stopped for Platt, and then both of them went on
to pick up Paulhan. While Platt was putting the body into the

cutter, Smead found the dead man's weaving trail and followed it back to the barn. He said nothing when he returned, nor even during the drive to Warrensburg, but from Estes' funeral parlor he telephoned for Harned, the village coroner.

When Harned arrived, Smead took him aside and told him as much as he knew about the case. They came back to where Platt was sitting and fell upon him like a roof. They slugged away until his chair toppled over and dumped him on the floor, and then they gave him leather, booting him all the way across the room and up against a wall. He fought back quietly until Smead dropped him with the butt of his revolver.

Harned put a call through to Jessup, the County Prosecutor, and insisted on his coming up from Lake George at once. By this time Estes had spread the news, and long before Jessup reached Warrensburg the funeral parlor was jammed with townsmen, and there was an overflow outside that blocked the highway. Estes' place was so small, and so many people wanted to witness the proceedings, that Smead transferred the hearing to the Grange Hall, which was directly across the road.

Jessup drove up as the last of the crowd was entering the Hall. After a short conference with Harned and Smead, he went up to the little platform and called the meeting to order.

The first witness to be called was Grace Paulhan, but she refused to testify. "I have nothing to say," she said.

"But all I want you to do, ma'am, is identify the body," Jessup said.

"I have nothing to say."

Estes was called.

"How long have you lived in Warrensburg?" Jessup said.

"All my life."

"Did you ever know a Thomas Liggett Paulhan?"

"Sure."

"Did Sheriff Smead bring a body to your funeral parlor this afternoon?"

"Yes."

"Whose body was it?"

"Tom Paulhan's."

"That's all."

Smead was the next witness. After being sworn, he said: "I got a call from Aaron Platt around noontime. He said he was over to Bertrand's, and he wanted me to come out to his farm right away—there was a dead man laying out in the road. I hitched up and drove out to Bertrand's, so's Platt could show me where the body was. We found it in the county road that leads past Platt's farm and up around the back of Harrington Hill to Luzerne. The place was about four miles from town, maybe a little over. That road being hardly ever used even in the summertime, I couldn't figure out how anybody happened to be coming down off of it in weather like today, specially Paulhan, because he hasn't been around these parts in five years or more. I went back over his trail for a ways and found out that he wasn't coming from Luzerne at all. His footprints only followed the road to just about opposite Platt's barn, and there they went over a fence and up onto Platt's west meadow. They crossed that and twisted along to the back door of the barn. I took a look inside . . . ."

"How many sets of prints did you find?"

"One."

"So that nobody was with Paulhan when he came from the barn, crossed the field, and started down the road?"

"If you mean was Platt with him—no. On my way back to the cutter, I found Platt's trail, but he'd come from the kitchen, and the two sets of footprints didn't join up till the spot where he run onto Paulhan's body."

"You say you looked into the barn. What did you find there?"

"Somebody'd been staying in one of the stalls."

"How do you know?"

"I'll have to talk kind of plain."

"The plainer the better."

"Well, as I said, somebody must of been living in that stall for quite a few days. It stank pretty bad—like an outhouse."

"Did you find anything else that made you think the stall had been used by a human being?"

"The straw was all packed down in one place, like a man'd been laying in it, and there was a big dark patch up towards one end that looked like dried blood."

"What did you do after leaving the barn?"

"I went back to my cutter. The body'd been loaded in by Platt, and he was waiting for me. We come right on in to town."

"And when you got to town?"

"I called Harned on the phone. He joined me over to Estes' place, and I told him what I found out."

"And then?"

"We both got sore."

"Yes?"

"And we kicked the shit out of Platt."

"You did, eh! By what right?"

"Well, we're both officers of the law."

"And that gave you the right to assault a prisoner?"

"Not exactly, but he didn't have any right to do what he done to Tom Paulhan."

"How do you know what he did to Paulhan?"

"It was right there in the snow. Christ, a blind man could of read that kind of sign!"

"Step down, Sherlock Holmes."

"What do you mean—step down?"

"Get to hell out of that chair—that's what I mean!"

Smead was followed by Doctor Slocum.

"Doctor," Jessup said, "did you examine the body of Thomas Paulhan when you were called to Estes' funeral parlor?"

"Yes."

"What was the cause of death?"

"Technically, Paulhan was frozen to death."

"Technically?"

"I mean freezing was the immediate cause."

"How many causes were there?"

"Quite a few."

"Name them."

"Starvation, for one."

"How long would you say Paulhan had gone without food?"

"At least a week, maybe ten days."

"So you'd say he died of starvation and exposure."

"There's more to it than that. At the time he died, he was suffering from two diseases. One of them was consumption."

"And the other?"

"I'd sooner not say."

"Why?"

"Because it's nobody's God damn business."

"That's for me to decide. Did this disease have anything to do with Paulhan's death?"

"I don't think so."

"You're a doctor. You ought to be sure."

"Only fools are sure."

"I want the facts, Slocum. Did this disease that you won't name have anything to do with Paulhan's death?"

"I told you before that I didn't think so."

"Would it have killed him later on?"

"Yes."

"How much later?"

"You never know."

"A month?"

"Maybe."

"A year?"

"You might start caving in any time at all."

"You refuse to tell the name of the disease?"

"Absolutely."

"One thing more—how do you know he had it? You couldn't have examined Paulhan very carefully."

"You can always tell."

"The other sickness, now—consumption. Is that what killed Paulhan?"

"I don't think so."

"My God, aren't you sure of anything?"

"I'm only a doctor. The way you fire questions at me, anybody'd think I was a God damn wizard."

"It doesn't take a wizard to tell whether a man died from consumption. Smead testified that Paulhan had a hemorrhage."

"Did he? I didn't hear him say that."

"How about that dried blood in the straw?"

"Who said it *was* dried blood?"

"Smead."

"Your memory's going back on you. He said it *looked* like dried blood."

"Suppose Paulhan'd been given food while he was in the barn, and suppose the place had been kept warm—do you think he'd have died when he did?"

"Hard to say."

"Why?"

"Because he died in the snow, not in the barn. What did you bring me up here for—to make guesses? If that's what you want, yours are as good as mine."

"Listen, Slocum—do you know Aaron Platt?"

"I know everybody in Warrensburg."

"I mean do you know him personally?"

"Yes."

"Do you like him?"

"What's that got to do with the case?"

"I'm asking the questions. Do you like Aaron Platt?"

"I never found anything to *dis*like him for."

"Do you *like* him?"

"Yes, I do, if you really want to know."

"I thought so, Doctor. That'll be all."

"You found out that I happen to like Platt, so you don't want to ask me any more questions. Is that it?"

"Step down, please."

"Maybe I'd make a better witness if I hated the sight of him."

"Step down!"

The Hall was very quiet for several seconds after Slocum had left the platform.

"Aaron Platt," Jessup said, "take the witness chair."

Platt went up to Jessup's table and sat down facing the crowd.

"This is only a preliminary hearing, Platt," Jessup said. "The purpose of it is to find out whether you should be held for the action of the Grand Jury. Do you understand?"

"Yes."

"Do you also understand that if you *are* held, the Grand Jury will be asked to return an indictment against you for murder?"

"Yes."

"And you know that you don't have to testify here if you don't want to?"

"Yes."

"And you know that you're entitled to be represented by counsel?"

"Yes."

"Do you want time to get yourself a lawyer?"

"No."

"I have to warn you, then, that anything you say here may be used as evidence against you later."

"God damn it, ask your questions, man!" Platt said. "What the hell do you want to know?"...

✤ ✤ ✤

Platt: ... I don't know where he got the strength to pick himself up and go off down the road, and to tell you the truth, I don't much care. All I know is that I was damn glad he didn't die on my land; if he did, he'd of poisoned it. And I'm glad he's dead too. I *wanted* him to die. The minute I set eyes on him that morning in the barn, I knew he was sick and starving, and if I didn't kick him out on his prat then and there, it was only account of his wife, but when he cut loose and begin raving about the kind of a life he'd been living, I couldn't help stacking it up against my own—him playing and me working, him playing and me working—and then I forgot all about his wife, and I didn't want him to go on living any more. I wanted him to *die,* and I *let* him die.

I done it on purpose. I done it because he was a nogood sonofabitch. I done it because for the first time in my life it was in my power to see a man get the justice that was coming to him—and right here on earth. If there'd of been a God you could depend on, my father and Paulhan would of been dead a long ways back, but Mister Titus' God is all a fake, and I finally come to realize it when Paulhan put himself at my mercy. For five days there, *I* was God as far as he was concerned.

Doc Slocum was trying to be nice when he held back his evidence. He was sorry for me, maybe. He thought I was just some poor devil that was all tore up account of nobody in town didn't want to have any truck with me. He was sorry for me, and so he tried to cover up the truth. But I don't appreciate that. I want everybody to get the straight of what I done.

I let Paulhan starve. I let him lay there in the bitter cold, knowing full well he was sick as a dog, knowing he needed attention, knowing he'd die if he didn't get it right away. I could of called in Slocum if I wanted to. If Paulhan was anybody else, I guess it wouldn't of worked so much hardship on me to of got to a phone five days sooner than what I done—but he *wasn't* anybody else. He was only the kind of a man I been telling you about all afternoon, and that kind just don't make me cry any more. He had everything in the world to live for, but he took his whole life and dumped it in the privy, and Grace Tennent's life along with it. He had everything I ever wanted, and look what he went and done with it.

You think I should of took him in with open arms? If so, that's the best joke I ever heard, and the further it goes, the funnier it's going to get—but even a good joke can go too far, and for my part I've got plenty of it right now. There's a lot of things that want doing up to the farm, so if Mister Jessup's all done looking up the law in that book of his, I'll thank him to tell me just where I stand.

❧ ❧ ❧

Jessup was not reading law when Platt finished his story; he was merely staring at the opened Penal Code. After a moment he removed his spectacles, idly ticking the frames against the edge of the table.

"Well?" Polhemus said.

Jessup looked up slowly. "I'm afraid you people brought me up here for nothing."

The word *nothing* rebounded from the rafters. No one spoke. No one moved.

"I'm afraid you people brought me up here for nothing," Jessup repeated.

Polhemus stood up. "You mean you can't find any crime in that book to pin onto Platt?"

"Yes," Jessup said, "that's what I mean."

The quiet was suddenly battered to bits by an assaulting roar. Polhemus went up to Jessup's table and pounded on it with his stick until he could make himself heard.

"Are you going to sit there and tell us it's the law of this state that a man can let somebody die of starvation and cold without being held to account for it? Is *that* what the law says?"

"It doesn't say *anything*, Polhemus, and in New York no man's act is a crime unless there's a particular provision for it in the Code."

"I don't believe it," Polhemus said. "You can't tell me the law lets a man go scotfree for murder!"

"Platt didn't murder Paulhan."

"No? What *did* he do, then?"

"Exactly what he said—he let him die."

"I never heard such horseshit in my life! Platt killed Paulhan the same as if he walked up and blew his head off with a shotgun. He killed him in cold blood, and if you say he didn't, then I'm damned if we need a Prosecutor in this county!"

"You brought me up here to tell you the law, and that's what I'm doing. Platt hasn't committed a crime."

"You're on his side—that's what you are! And if you want my personal opinion, it don't smell so good from where I'm standing."

"Why, you God damn whorehouse keeper—I don't know this Platt from a hole in the ground!"

"You're going to find a crime to hang onto him, or else you're going to stand out of our way when we take him along to somebody that will."

"Listen, you old snort—let any man lay a finger on Platt, and I'll see to it that he's indicted for assault and battery so damn fast he'll see double!"

Platt rose from his chair. "I guess I'll be going along," he said.

There was no sound from the mob as he stepped from the platform and went up the aisle between the two banks of benches. Looking at no one, he seemed to be concerned only with buttoning the collar of his sheepskin mackinaw. The links of his open galoshes jingled as he walked.

"Wait a minute, you!" Polhemus shouted as Platt neared the last row of benches. "You're not going to walk out of here as pretty as all that!"

Platt slowly turned to face him. "Try and stop me," he said, "and I'll knock the trotters out from under you. You made your last trouble for me, you old fart—I give you fair warning."

Polhemus threw his stick away and strode up the aisle. "You murderer!" he said, and he grabbed Platt's arm.

Platt's fist hit Polhemus like a sack of tools. It clanked on his face, and he went down like a suit of armor. The blow smashed the plates of his false teeth, hammering the rough edges of the vulcanized rubber deep into his cheeks and gums. Bloody mangled flesh and bits of broken plate crawled from his mouth like the survivors of a wreck.

From the floor, he cried, "Men, let him get out of this Hall, and you're no better than what he is! He's a murderer whether the law says so or not, and he's got to be punished like a murderer!"

"Arrest Polhemus!" Jessup said to Smead.

"In the face of that mob? Not me, I don't."

"Who are your deputies?"

"Confrey and Robbins."

"Confrey!" Jessup called out. "Confrey!"

"What's eating you, lawyer?" Confrey said.

"Arrest Polhemus!"

"What for, lawyer?"

"Committing a battery on Platt."

"On *Platt!* Why, Platt hit *him!*"

"Robbins!" Jessup shouted. "Where's Robbins?"

"Right here, sir," said a man near the door.

"Put Polhemus under arrest, God damn it!"

"Yes, sir," Robbins said, and he walked straight into the mob. He was knocked off his feet and buried before he got within ten yards of the old man.

The mob picked up Platt and rushed him toward the door as if he were a battering ram. They slowed up going through, and then they flowed out over the snow, leaving Jessup, Smead, and Slocum standing at the table, leaving Polhemus hanging over the back of a bench and Robbins lying on the floor. Robbins, trampled on by half the crowd, pulled himself up and dragged toward Polhemus.

"Come on, Smead!" Jessup cried. "They'll kill him out there!"

"I'm staying here. He *ought* to get killed."

Jessup rushed to the doorway, but stopped dead when he reached it. "Come here, Doc," he said. "Take a look."

Slocum joined him at the door. The crowd was bunched in a loose fist of figures directly in front of the Hall. Twenty feet away stood Platt. In between, scattered on the snow, lay all his clothes except his underwear.

"Start walking," someone said.

Platt turned, and as he moved off down the road a hard-packed snowball caught him in the small of his back. Part of the snowball clung to the nap of the underwear, the white polkadot so merging with the white landscape beyond that a great hole seemed to have been drilled through Platt's body. Then a cloud of snowballs fell upon him like a troop of hungry birds.

"And *keep* walking!"

⚜ ⚜ ⚜

At every house along the two miles of road between the Grange Hall and Bertrand's, Platt's arrival was awaited by those who had been unable to attend the hearing. They were silent when he came into sight, and they were silent as he passed by, and then they sped him on his way with rocks of snow until he was out of range.

Platt stopped short when he was hidden from the last house by a bend in the road. He stopped as if detained by a sudden recollection, and for a moment he stood motionless, letting the thought flood him, and then slowly he looked down as his fingers began to pluck at the stiff fibers of his unionsuit.

The late afternoon was soundless, and there was no wind to slant the fall of the lilac snow. No birds flew in the dead air, and no animals ran upon the dead earth, and Platt's long vibrating laugh shimmered away and died like a tuningfork struck in a great empty room. He cut into the forest and headed downhill toward a little house near Thurman bridge.

Still dressed in a heavy coat, Grace Paulhan opened the door in answer to his knock, and for several seconds neither of them spoke. Slowly she inspected him, from the frosting on his head to the boots of ice that had formed on the legs of his underwear.

"I just remembered today was Saturday," he said.

"Yes?"

"So I come to pay you a little call."

"Yes?"

"Only this time I want my dollar's worth."

Again the woman's eyes made a slow tour of his body, and then she opened the door a little wider. Platt started forward, but she put her hand against his chest and blocked him.

"Where's the dollar?" she said.

"In my pants, laying in the road over by the Grange Hall. I'll pay you double next week."

"Come in, customer," she said, letting her hand fall.

FROM WHARTON'S
CRIMINAL LAW

SECTION 455: We have already seen that an omission is not the basis of penal action unless it constitutes a defect in the discharge of a responsibility specially imposed. And the converse is true, that when a lawful duty is imposed upon a party, then an omission on his part in the discharge of such duty, which affects injuriously the party to whom the duty is owed, is an indictable offense.

SECTION 456: As, in conformity with the definition just stated, the responsibility must be one specially imposed on the defendant, the omission to perform acts of mercy, even though death to another result from such omission, is not within the rule. *One man, for instance, may see another starving, and may be able, without the least inconvenience to himself, to bring food to the sufferer, and thus save the latter's life; but the omission to do so is not indictable,* unless there be a special responsibility to this effect imposed upon the defendant.

Burrell vs State: 18 Texas 713
Connaughty vs State: 1 Wisc. 159
Rex vs Smith: 1 Car. & P. 449
People vs Smith: 56 Misc. 1

AFTERWORD
BY JACK MEARNS

Make My Bed in Hell is as finely written a novel as one could hope to read. Gripping in its plot, and intricately narrated with interweaving voices, it delves deeply into man's moral responsibility to aid another in distress—even when the sufferer has caused a lifetime of resentment in the one who could offer care. *Make My Bed in Hell* can be read on one level as a brisk, gritty depiction of crime and punishment. But it goes beyond simple courtroom drama to echo the biblical question: how many times can one be insulted and abused and still be expected to forgive?

Make My Bed in Hell is the centerpiece of John Sanford's Warrensburg trilogy—set in the fictionalized village in New York's Adirondack Mountains—each successive book of which charts Sanford's own moral and political awakening during the tumultuous years of the Great Depression. With each new novel, Sanford bored more deeply into the troubled soul of America, hidden beneath the idyllic veneer of small-town life. Each new novel more explicitly linked violence and inequity in modern America to the arrival of Europeans on the continent—their befouling the land and waters, their decimating the indigenous populace, and their importing enslaved Africans as captive labor. Digging ever deeper into the life of this mountain hamlet enabled Sanford to more expansively chronicle America at large, confirming *Regionalism in America's* author, Benjamin Spencer's, statement: "Human nature is everywhere the same, and the faithful portrayal of an obscure provincial contains the universal story."

John Sanford's birth name was Julian Shapiro. The child of immigrants from Eastern Europe, he was born in an elegant brick apartment building in Harlem, NY, that overlooked Mt. Morris Park. By Sanford's 1904 birth, his father had prospered as lawyer, sealing deals among developers, builders and property owners in the flourishing Jewish community. However, the elegance of *The Gainsboro* building did not last long, as the financial panic of 1907 and the mother's chronic illness devastated the family's finances. When Sanford was ten years old, his mother died, and Sanford fell into a listless intransigence. He rebelled against his father and, though his mother had fostered a love of learning, he lost interest in school.

It was not until 1924 that Sanford finally turned his life around by resolving to join his father in the legal profession. Sanford enrolled in Fordham Law School in downtown Manhattan, whose classes met in the Woolworth tower, at the time the tallest building in the world. Though he would go on to complete his law degree and join the bar, Sanford's legal career was derailed by a 1925 encounter with a figure from his Harlem youth. On a New Jersey golf course, Sanford recognized a gawky solo golfer as Nathan Weinstein; however, Weinstein was now calling himself Nathanael West. When Sanford bragged that he was becoming a lawyer, West replied that he was writing a book. The idea of writing a book transfixed Sanford, and lawyering forever lost its appeal.

West and Sanford became frequent companions back in New York. During long walks around the city, West schooled Sanford about art and literature, introducing him to modernists like James Joyce and Ernest Hemingway. To make up for the years of intellectual paralysis after his mother's death, Sanford put himself on a crash course in reading. Though Sanford passed the bar and joined his father's firm, literature remained his passion. In fact, his autobiographical first novel, 1933's *The Water Wheel*, has as its protagonist a New York lawyer who dreams of becoming a writer. The character's name? John Sanford.

After the 1929 stock market crash, there was less and less legal work to distract Sanford from writing. He began to place short pieces in avant-garde literary "little magazines." In the summer of 1931, he and West holed up in a rented hunting lodge in the Adirondack Mountains, at Viele Pond near the town of Warrensburg. West worked on *Miss Lonelyhearts* and Sanford revised *The Water Wheel*. That summer deepened the New Yorker's appreciation for nature and imbued him with the pace of life of the bucolic region.

Sanford's first novels display his development as a writer, both as a wordsmith and as a commentator on America. The autobiographical *Water Wheel* was self-consciously artistic. Owing much to Joyce, its language and punctuation are unconventional. Although told in the third person, the narration is obsessively focused on the mind of the novel's feckless and emotionally wrought anti-hero. The novel showed flashes of brilliance but had no chance of mass appeal.

For his 1935 follow-up, Sanford clearly strove to write a book that would sell, just as William Faulkner claimed to have done with *Sanctuary*. *The Old Man's Place* is a barn-burner of a tale about the spree of mayhem unleashed when a trio of World War One veterans returns to the farm on which one of them was raised. The prose is vigorous and spare, and the plot unfolds rapidly and mercilessly. While *The Water Wheel* was self-absorbed and had ambitions to high art, *The Old Man's Place* is objective in its narrative viewpoint, amoral in its ethos, and intended to move copies off the shelf. In an extra effort to boost sales, Sanford adopted his *Water Wheel* protagonist's name as a pseudonym; for the rest of his career, he would write as John Sanford.

The Old Man's Place sold only a little over 1,000 copies. But, as there were no clients demanding legal services to divert his attention from writing, Sanford embarked on his third novel. He based it on a short story, "I Let Him Die," that he had published in *Pagany* in 1932. A farmer finds a man he knows from his youth freezing to death in his barn. Rather than offering aid or seeking help, the farmer allows the man to die. An inquest follows at which the farmer explains his motive—resentment at the interloper's vagabond life, while the farmer has broken his back to scratch a living from his played-out, rocky fields. In the novel, Sanford filled in the back stories of the characters and added a broader social element. With the addition of a blank verse section covering American history, Sanford roots the farmer's willful neglect in the inequity and iniquity inflicted on the continent since Europeans' arrival.

Before he could make much progress on the new novel, however, on the basis of *The Old Man's Place*, Sanford was summoned to Hollywood as a screenwriter. He worked for a year at Paramount Studios, but he produced no script that made it to the screen and was let go. The most important event during his time at Paramount was meeting Marguerite "Maggie" Roberts, an up-and-coming screenwriter. Roberts and Sanford soon became a couple, and Sanford would write much of *Make My Bed in Hell* in the back yard of Roberts's San Fernando Valley home.

Originally published as *Seventy Times Seven* but reissued in pulp paperbacks in the 1950's as *Make My Bed in Hell*, the novel reveals Sanford at the height of his creative powers. The plot is simple yet powerful, expanding his original story. Sanford's narrative structure interweaves multiple voices, each telling a portion of the tale. There is the straightforward reporting of events by Aaron Platt, the owner of the farm. There are the delirious ramblings of Tom Paulhan, the trespasser who will soon die. And there is the testimony at the inquest following Paulhan's death. In his own testimony, Platt recounts his personal history to explain his actions. As a child, he was terrorized by a brutal father and bullied and ostracized by other kids, led by Paulhan. As an adult, Platt brims with resentment over Paulhan's carefree life of irresponsibility, compared to Platt's Sisyphean life of toil—"him playing and me working." The novel deftly addresses universal themes by delving into the relationships among the townspeople.

Sanford also connects the actions of the individual characters to the national character by adding a fourth narrative voice that recounts America's blood-soaked past. From an early age, Sanford was fascinated by history. One of the few possessions he retained from his wandering youth was a child's history of the United States given him by his mother, *Patriotic America*. In *The Water Wheel*, Sanford had included a lengthy passage about Philip Nolan, the Man Without a Country. But in *Make My Bed in Hell*, Sanford explicitly entwined the contemporary narrative with the nation's violent history—asserting that the actions of specific Americans today cannot be separated from the conduct of Europeans since they first set foot on North America. Sanford accomplished this with a long blank verse poem largely about whites' warfare with native peoples. In the novel, Platt says of his deceased tyrannical father: "Why he was stronger dead than most people are when they're alive!" In fact, Platt appears to be the town pariah simply because he is the son of a despised man. The influence of the past is inescapable: the denizens of Warrensburg are "knee deep in history"—in the blood that "fill[s] the open sewer of America." Sanford suggests Warrensburg's small-town folk are doomed to live out the legacy not only of their own fathers but of the generations of plunderers and enslavers from which white America has descended.

In the books that followed *Make My Bed in Hell*, Sanford would continue to quarry American history to build the foundation for his fiction. In 1943's *The People from Heaven*, he interleaved historical episodes within the narrative, starting with

Columbus's discovery of the New World. Sanford carried on this practice in *A Man without Shoes* (1951) and *The Land that Touches Mine* (1953). Eventually Sanford gave up fiction, devoting himself entirely to evocations of history. Starting in the 1970's, Sanford published five volumes wholly comprising personal interpretations of historical events and characters.

By the time *Make My Bed in Hell* was published, Sanford had joined the screenwriters' wing of the Communist Party. Clearly, the humanism—the sympathy and outrage about the abused and disadvantaged—that attracted Sanford to the Party is on display in *Make My Bed in Hell*. However, *Make My Bed in Hell* remains free of the explicit Communist ideology that would make his succeeding novels more overtly political, at times at the expense of their quality as fiction.

Sanford's cousin Mel Friedman shopped *Make My Bed in Hell* around New York, where it was rejected by several prominent publishers. The rejections were in part due to the blank verse section, which some reviewers found irrelevant or causing an abrupt cessation of the action of the plot. Finally, the novel was accepted by Knopf, which also suggested removing the historical verse and "pruning" certain sections an editor considered over-written. Sanford refused to make these edits—although, in his autobiography decades later, he rued not having followed the editor's suggestions. In hindsight, he agreed that these passages could have been cleaner, making them more effective: "Less is more," his idol William Carlos Williams had told him.

Despite Sanford's obdurateness, Knopf kept the book. They even arranged with Constable to release it in England. However, Sanford rejected Constable's stipulation to remove the verse passage and other "objectionable material." This stubbornness cost him a U.K. release. At the end of 1938, Sanford and Roberts headed east for rehearsals of Maggie's star-crossed stage play *Farewell Performance*. They had a City Hall wedding in downtown Manhattan. In March of 1939, the Sanfords were in Boston for the play's trial run, when Sanford spotted copies of *Make My Bed in Hell* on display in a bookstore window.

As with *The Old Man's Place*, some reviewers found *Make My Bed in Hell* too gritty. *Kirkus Reviews* wrote: "An unusual book with some pieces of brilliant writing, but also with some of the most bestial and flamboyantly crude passages ever encountered on the printed page, exceeding Celine and Faulkner in depravity and language.... A ruthless, repellant book." The Los Angeles *Times* erroneously referred to the novel as Sanford's first but accurately perceived Sanford's aim, expressing particular appreciation for the historic section: "He is filled with ideas and tried to get the whole of America into a brief, fast book of less than 200 pages, and those pages terse.... Sanford has injected the drama of spilled blood that made America... [in] a long blank-verse section of tremendous power." The New York *Times* wrote: "The prose is fresh and energetic, the storytelling superb, and the writing comes out raw and terrifying as an exposed nerve.... This novel stands high as a piece of realistic writing...[with] stylistic variety that few authors now writing can manage."

Farewell Performance closed during previews in Boston, and the couple returned to California. Roberts had a contract at Metro-Goldwyn-Mayer awaiting her. She would soon write A-list pictures for the studio's biggest stars. In 1941, Sanford joined Roberts for his only screenwriting credit—the Clark Gable/Lana Turner comedic Western, *Honky Tonk*. After the film's success, M-G-M offered Sanford employment, too, but Maggie urged him to turn the job down. She would thereafter bankroll him as he wrote "our books."

Sanford went on to finish the Warrensburg trilogy with 1943's *The People from Heaven*. Under the terms of his contract, he submitted it to Knopf, which rejected the book. Several publishers followed suit, citing its highly experimental style as too taxing for potential readers: "We feel the book is a mistake...too difficult to read, to understand, and to sell." "You've combined so many experimental techniques that...even a better than average reader would come up with a feeling of frustration." When the book was finally published by Harcourt, Brace, reviewers complained that it was "entirely too abstract for the purposes of fiction" and "one of the most unconventional works of fiction since James Joyce's *Ulysses.*"

Make My Bed in Hell represents a sweet spot in Sanford's growth as a novelist, the summation of experience culled from writing his previous books but not yet pushing the boundaries of fiction so hard as to risk losing the majority of readers. We can see in *Make My Bed in Hell* elements from his other work: the vigorous, lean prose of *The Old Man's Place* in the main narration and Platt's testimony; *The Water Wheel's* impressionistic stream of consciousness in Paulhan's delirium, such as his rapturous description of the lights of New York City; and *The People from Heaven's* obsession with the historic roots of America's dark underbelly. *Make My Bed in Hell* showcases the best of John Sanford's diverse skills, with the whole exceeding the sum of its parts.

Both in terms of story-telling and the keenness of the writing, I consider *Make My Bed in Hell* to be Sanford's most accomplished novel. It achieves being a work of art less self-consciously than his other fiction, while not cheating plot and character. *Make My Bed in Hell* is not just a book about ideas. It is a powerfully written, intensely compelling book about people's relationships and the burdens of the past they bear. Ultimately it presents a paradoxical message, on the one hand arguing, like Camus, for the indomitability of the human spirit, while on the other hand concluding the futility of community, fellowship and love. Such are the dividends of the hatred on which the nation was founded. *Make My Bed in Hell* has been too long out of print. It is most welcome that Brash Books has put this entertaining and edifying novel before the public again.

Books by John Sanford

Novels and Stories
1933: *The Water Wheel*, Dragon (reissued 2020 by Tough Poets)

1935: *The Old Man's Place*, Albert & Charles Boni (reissued 1953 by Permabooks; 1957 as *The Hard Guys* by Signet; 2021 by Brash)

1939: *Seventy Times Seven*, Knopf (reissued 1954 & 1957 as *Make My Bed in Hell* by Avon; 2021 by Brash as *Make My Bed in Hell*)

1943: *The People from Heaven*, Harcourt, Brace (reissued 1995 by University of Illinois)

1951: *A Man Without Shoes*, Plantin (reissued 1982 by Black Sparrow; 2013 by Bloomsbury Reader [e-book])

1953: *The Land that Touches Mine*, Doubleday & Jonathan Cape

1964: *Every Island Fled Away*, Norton

1967: *The $300 Man*, Prentice-Hall

1976: *Adirondack Stories*, Capra

Creative Interpretations of History
1975: *A More Goodly Country*, Horizon

1977: *View from this Wilderness*, Capra

1980: *To Feed Their Hopes*, University of Illinois (reissued 1995 as *A Book of American Women* by University of Illinois)

1984: *The Winters of that Country*, Black Sparrow

1997: *Intruders in Paradise*, University of Illinois

Autobiography, Memoir and Letters
1984: *William Carlos Williams/John Sanford: A Correspondence*, Oyster

1985: *The Color of the Air*, Black Sparrow

1986: *The Waters of Darkness*, Black Sparrow

1987: *A Very Good Land to Fall With*, Black Sparrow

1989: *A Walk in the Fire*, Black Sparrow

1991: *The Season, It Was Winter*, Black Sparrow

1993: *Maggie: A Love Story*, Barricade (reissued 2013 by Bloomsbury Reader [e-book])

1994: *The View from Mt. Morris*, Barricade

1995: *We Have a Little Sister*, Capra

2003: *A Palace of Silver*, Capra (reissued 2013 by Bloomsbury Reader [e-book])

2021: *Speaking in an Empty Room: The Selected Letters of John Sanford*, Tough Poets

Jack Mearns is a professor of psychology at California State University, Fullerton. He is the author of *John Sanford: An Annotated Bibliography* (Oak Knoll Press, 2008).

Made in the USA
Las Vegas, NV
11 December 2021

36846027R00111